COUNT BUNKER

BEING

A BALD YET VERACIOUS CHRONICLE CONTAINING
SOME FURTHER PARTICULARS OF TWO GENTLEMEN
WHOSE PREVIOUS CAREERS WERE TOUCHED UPON
IN A TOME ENTITLED "THE LUNATIC AT LARGE"

BY

J. STORER CLOUSTON

BRENTANO'S
NEW YORK
1907

COUNT BUNKER

CHAPTER I

IT is only with the politest affectation of interest, as a rule, that English Society learns the arrival in its midst of an ordinary Continental nobleman; but the announcement that the Baron Rudolph von Blitzenberg had been appointed attache to the German embassy at the Court of St. James was unquestionably received with a certain flutter of excitement. That his estates were as vast as an average English county, and his ancestry among the noblest in Europe, would not alone perhaps have arrested the attention of the para-graphists, since acres and forefathers of foreign extraction are rightly regarded as conferring at the most a claim merely to toleration. But in addition to these he possessed a charming English wife, belonging to one of the most distinguished families in the peerage (the Grill-yers of Monkton-Grillyer), and had further demonstrated his judgment by purchasing the winner of the last year's Derby, with a view to improving the horseflesh of his native land.

From a footnote attached to the engraving of the Baron in a Homburg hat holding the head of the steed
in question, which formed the principal attraction in several print-sellers' windows in Piccadilly, one gathered that though his faculties had been cultivated and exercised in every conceivable direction, yet this was his first serious entrance into the diplomatic world. There was clearly, therefore, something unusual about the appointment ; so that it was rumored, and rightly, that an international importance was to be attached to the incident, and a delicate compliment to be perceived in the selection of so popular a link between the Anglo-Saxon and the Teutonic peoples. Accordingly " Die Wacht am Rhein " was played by the Guards' band down the entire length of Ebury Street, photographs of the Baroness appeared in all the leading periodicals, and Society, after its own less demonstrative but equally sincere fashion, prepared to welcome the distinguished visitors.

They arrived in town upon a delightful day in July, somewhat late in the London season, to be sure, yet not too late to be inundated with a snowstorm of cards and invitations to all the smartest functions that remained. For the first few weeks, at least, you would suppose the Baron to have no time for thought beyond official receptions and unofficial dinners; yet as he looked from his drawing-room windows into the gardens of Belgrave Square upon the second afternoon since they had settled into this great mansion, it was not upon such functions that his fancy ran. Nobody was more fond of gaiety, nobody more appreciative of purple and fine linen, than the Baron von Blitzenberg; but as he mused there he began to recall more and more vividly, and with an ever
rising pleasure, quite different memories of life in London. Then by easy stages regret began to cloud this reminiscent satisfaction, until at last he sighed—

" Ach, my dear London! How moch should I enjoy you if I were free! "

For the benefit of those who do not know the Baron either personally or by repute, he may briefly be described as an admirably typical Teuton. When he first visited England (some five years previously) he stood for Bavarian manhood in the flower; now, you behold the fruit. As magnificently mustached, as ruddy of skin, his eye as genial, and his impulses as hearty; he added to-day to these two more stone of Teutonic excellences incarnate.

In his ingenuous glance, as in the more rounded contour of his waistcoat, you could see at once that fate had dealt kindly with him. Indeed, to hear him sigh was so unwonted an occurrence that the Baroness looked up with an air of mild surprise.

" My dear Rudolph," said she, " you should really open the window. You are evidently feeling the heat."

" No, not ze heat," replied the Baron.

He did not turn his head towards her, and she looked at him more anxiously.

" What is it, then? I have noticed a something strange about you ever since we landed at Dover. Tell me, Rudolph!"

Thus adjured, he cast a troubled glance in her direction. He saw a face whose mild blue eyes and undetermined mouth he still swore by as the standard by which to try all her inferior sisters, and a figure whose growing embonpoint yearly approached the outline of his ideal hausfrau. But it was either St. Anthony or one of his fellow-martyrs who observed that an occasional holiday from the ideal is the condiment in the sauce of sanctity; and some such reflection perturbed the Baron at this moment.

" It is nozing moch," he answered.

" Oh, I know what it is. You have grown so accustomed to seeing the same people, year after year—the Von Greifners, and Rosenbaums, and all those. You miss them, don't you? Personally, I think it a very good thing that you should go abroad and be a diplomatist, and not stay in Fogelschloss so much; and you'll soon make loads of friends here. Mother comes to us next week, you know."

" Your mozzer is a nice old lady," said the Baron slowly. " I respect her, Alicia; bot it vas not mozzers zat I missed just now."

" What was it? "

" Life! " roared the Baron, with a sudden outburst of thundering enthusiasm that startled the Baroness completely out of her composure. " I did have fun for my money vunce in London. Himmel, it is too hot to eat great dinners and to vear clothes like a monkey-j ack."

" Like a what? " gasped the Baroness.

To hear the Baron von Blitzenberg decry the paraphernalia and splendors of his official liveries was even more astonishing than his remarkable denunciation of the pleasures of the table, since to dress as well as play the part of hereditary grandee had been till this minute his constant and enthusiastic ambition.

" A meat-jack, I mean—or a—I know not vat you call it. Ach, I vant a leetle fun, Alicia."

" A little fun," repeated the Baroness in a breathless voice. " What kind of fun? "

" I know not," said he, turning once more to stare out of the window.

To this dignified representative of a particularly dignified State even the trees of Belgrave Square seemed at that moment a trifle too conventionally perpendicular. If they would but dance and wave their boughs he would have greeted their greenness more gladly. A good-looking nursemaid wheeled a perambulator beneath their shade, and though she never looked his way, he took a wicked pleasure in surreptitiously closing first one eye and then the other in her direction. This might not entirely satisfy the aspirations of his soul, yet it seemed to serve as some vent for his pent-up spirit. He turned to his spouse with a pleasantly meditative air.

" I should like to see old Bonker vunce more," he observed.

" Bunker? You mean Mr. Mandell-Essington? " said she, with an apprehensive note in her voice.

" To me he vill alvays be Bonker."

The Baroness looked at him reproachfully.

" You promised me, Rudolph, you would see as little as possible of Mr. Essington."

" Oh, ja, as leetle —as possible," answered the Baron, though not with his most ingenuous air. " Besides, it is tree years since I promised. For tree years I have seen nozing. My love Alicia, you vould not have me forget mine friends altogezzer? "

But the Baroness had too vivid a recollection of their last (and only) visit to England since their marriage. By a curious coincidence that also was three years ago.

" When you last met you remember what happened? " she asked, with an ominous hint of emotion in her accents.

" My love, how often have I eggsplained? Zat night you mean, I did schleep in mine hat because I had got a cold in my head. I vas not dronk, no more zan you. Vat you found in my pocket vas a mere joke, and ze cabman who called next day vas jost vat I told him to his ogly face—a blackmail." "' You gave him money to go away."

" A Blitzenberg does not bargain mit cabmen," said the Baron loftily.

His wife's spirits began to revive. There seemed to speak the owner of Fogelschloss, the haughty magnate of Bavaria.

" You have too much self-respect to wish to find yourself in such a position again," she said. " I know you have, Rudolph!"

The Baron was silent. This appeal met with distinctly less response than she confidently counted upon. In a graver note she inquired—

" You know what mother thinks of Mr. Essington? "

" Your mozzer is a vise old lady, Alicia; but we do not zink ze same on all opinions."

" She will be exceedingly displeased if you—well, if you do anything that she thoroughly disapproves of."

The Baron left the window and took his wife's plump hand affectionately within his own broad palm.

" You can assure her, my love, zat I shall never do vat she dislikes. You vill say zat to her if she inquires ? "

"Can I, truthfully?"

" Ach, my own dear! "

From his enfolding arms she whispered tenderly—

" Of course I will, Rudolph! "

With a final hug the embrace abruptly ended, and the Baron hastily glanced at his watch.

" Ach, nearly had I forgot! I must go to ze club for half an hour."

"Must you?"

" To meet a friend."

" What friend? " asked the Baroness quickly.

" A man whose name you vould know veU—oh, vary veil known he is ! But in diplomacy, mine Alicia, a quiet meeting in a club is sometimes better not to be advertised too moch. Great wars have come from one vord of indiscretion. You know ze axiom of Bismarck— fi In diplomacy it is necessary for a diplomatist to be diplomatic.' Good-by, my love."

He bowed as profoundly as if she were a reigning sovereign, blew an affectionate kiss as he went through the door, and then descended the stairs with a rapidity that argued either that his appointment was urgent or that diplomacy shrank from a further test within this mansion.

CHAPTER II

FOR the last year or two the name of Rudolph von Blitzenberg had appeared in the members' list of that most exclusive of institutions, the Regent's Club, Pall Mall; and it was thither he drove on this fine afternoon of July. At no resort in London were more famous personages to be found, diplomatic and otherwise, and nothing would have been more natural than a meeting between the Baron and a European celebrity beneath its roof; so that if you had seen him bounding impetuously up the steps, and noted the eagerness with which he inquired whether a gentleman had called for him, you would have had considerable excuse for supposing his appointment to be with a dignitary of the highest importance.

" Goot! " he cried on learning that a stranger was indeed waiting for him. His face beamed with anticipatory joy. Aha! he was not to be disappointed.

" Vill he be jost the same? " he wondered. " Ah, if he is changed I shall veep! "

He rushed into the smoking-room, and there, instead of any bald notability or spectacled statesman, there advanced to meet him a merely private English gentleman, tolerably young, undeniably good-looking, and graced with the most debonair of smiles.

" My dear Bonker! " cried the Baron, crimsoning with joy. " Ach, how pleased I am,! "

" Baron! " replied his visitor gaily. " You cannot deceive me—that waistcoat was made in Germany! Let me lead you to a respectable tailor! "

Yet, despite his bantering tone, it was easy to see that he took an equal pleasure in the meeting.

" Ha, ha!" laughed the Baron, " vot a f onny zing to say! Droll as ever, eh? "

66 Five years less droll than when we first met," said the late Bunker and present Essington. " You meet a dullish dog, Baron—a sobered reveller."

" Ach, no! Not surely ? Do not disappoint me, dear Bonker!"

The Baron's plaintive note seemed to amuse his friend.

" You don't mean to say you actually wish a boon companion? You, Baron, the modern Talleyrand, the repository of three emperors' secrets? My dear fellow, I nearly came in deep mourning."

"Mourning! For vat?"

" For our lamented past: I supposed you would have the air of a Nonconformist beadle."

" My friend!" said the Baron eagerly, and yet with a lowering of his voice, " I vould not like to engage a beadle mit jost ze same feelings as me. Come here to zis corner and let us talk! Vaiter! whisky—soda— cigars—all for two. Come, Bonker ! "

Stretched in arm-chairs, in a quiet corner of the room, the two surveyed one another with affectionate and humorous interest. For three years they had not seen

one another at all, and save once they had not met for five. In five years a man may change his religion or lose his hair, inherit a principality or part with a reputation, grow a beard or turn teetotaler. Nothing so fundamental had happened to either of our friends. The Baron's fullness of contour we have already noticed; in Mandell-Essington, ex Bunker, was to be seen even less evidence of the march of time. But years, like wheels upon a road, can hardly pass without leaving in their wake some faint impress, however fair the weather, and perhaps his hair lay a fraction of an inch higher up the temple, and in the corners of his eyes a hint might even be discerned of those little wrinkles that register the smiles and frowns. Otherwise he was the same distinguished-looking, immaculately dressed, supremely self-possessed, and charming Francis Bunker, whom the Baron's memory stored among its choicer possessions.

" Tell me," demanded the Baron, " vat you are doing mit yourself, mine Bonker."

" Doing?" said Essington, lighting his cigar. " Well, my dear Baron, I am endeavoring to live as I imagine a gentleman should."

"And how is zat? "

" Riding a little, shooting a little, and occasionally telling the truth. At other times I cock a wise eye at my modest patrimony, now and then I deliver a lecture with magic-lantern slides; and when I come up to town I sometimes watch cricket-matches. A devilish invigorating programme, isn't it ? "

" Ha, ha!" laughed the Baron again; he had come prepared to laugh, and carried out his intention religiously. " But you do not feel more old and sober, eh? "

" I don't want to, but no man can avoid his destiny. The natives of this island are a serious people, or if they are frivolous, it is generally a trifle vulgarly done. The diversions of the professedly gay—hooting over pointless badinage and speculating whose turn it is to get divorced next—become in time even more sobering than a scientific study with diagrams of how to breed pheasants or play golf. If some one would teach us the simple art of being light-hearted he would deserve to be placed along with Nelson on his monument."

" Oh, my dear vellow! " cried the Baron. " Do I hear zese kind of vords from you ? "

" If you starved a city-full of people, wouldn't you expect to hear the man with the biggest appetite cry loudest?"

The Baron's face fell further and Essington laughed aloud.

" Come, Baron, hang it! You of all people should be delighted to see me a fellow-member of respectable society. I take you to be the type of the conventional aristocrat. Why, a fellow who's been travelling in Germany said to me lately, when I asked about you—* Von Blitzenberg,' said he, * he's used as a simile for traditional dignity. His very dogs have to sit up on their hind-legs when he inspects the kennels!' :

The Baron with a solemn face gulped down his whisky-and-soda.

"but

" Zat is not true about my dogs," he replied, I do confess my life is vary dignified. So moch is expected of a Blitzenberg. Oh, ja, zere is moch state and ceremony."

" And you seem to thrive on it."

" Veil, it does not destroy ze appetite," the Baron admitted ; " and it is my duty so to live at Fogelschlos and I alvays vish to do my duty. But, ach, sometimes do vant to kick ze trace! "

" You mean you would want to if it were not for the Baroness? "

Bunker smiled whimsically; but his friend continued as simply serious as ever.

" Alicia is ze most divine woman in ze world— I respect her, Bonker, I love her, I gonsider her my better angel; but even in Heaven, I suppose, peoples sometimes vould enjoy a stroll in Piccadeelly, or in some vay to exercise ze legs and shout mit excitement. No doubt you zink it unaccountable and strange—pairhaps ungrateful of me, eh? "

" On the contrary, I feel as I should if I feared this cigar had gone out and then found it alight after all."

" You say so! Ah, zen I will have more boldness to confess my heart! Bonker, ven I did land in England ze leetle thought zat vould rise vas—' Ze land of freedom vunce again! Here shall I not have to be alvays ze Baron von Blitzenberg, oldest noble in Bavaria, hereditary carpet-beater to ze Court! I vill disguise and go mit old Bonker for a frolic!' "

" You touch my tenderest chord, Baron! "

" Goot, goot, my friend! " cried the Baron, warming to his work of confession like a penitent whose absolution is promised in advance; " you speak ze vords I love to hear! Of course I vould not be vicked, and I vould not disgrace myself; but I do need a leetle exercise. Is it possible? "

Essington sprang up and enthusiastically shook his hand.

" Dear Baron, you come like a ray of sunshine through a London fog—like a moulin rouge alighting in Carlton House Terrace! I thought my own leaves were yellowing; I now perceive that was only an autumnal change. Spring has returned, and I feel like a green bay tree! "

" Hoch, hoch! " roared the Baron, to the great surprise of two Cabinet Ministers and a Bishop who were taking tea at the other side of the room. " Vat shall ve do to show zere is no sick feeling ? "

" H'm," reflected Essington, with a comical look. " There's a lot of scaffolding at the bottom of St. James's Street. Should we have it down to-night? Or what do you say to a packet of dynamite in the twopenny tube? "

The Baron sobered down a trifle.

" Ach, not so fast, not qvite so fast, dear Bonker. Remember I must not get into treble at ze embassy."

" My dear fellow, that's your pull. Foreign diplomatists are police-proof!"

"Ah, but my wife!"

" One stormy hour —then tears and forgiveness! "

COUNT BUNKER

The Baron lowered his voice.

" Her mozzer vill visit us next veek. I loff and respect Lady Grillyer; but I should not like to have to ask her for forgiveness."

" Yes, she has rather an uncompromising nose, so far as I remember."

" It is a kind nose to her friends, Bonker," the Baron explained, " but severe towards "

" Myself, for instance," laughed Essington. " Well, what do you suggest? "

" First, zat you dine mit me to-night. No, I vill take no refusal! Listen! I am now meeting a distinguished person on important international business—do you pairceive? Ha, ha, ha! To-night it vill be necessary ve most dine togezzer. I have an engagement, but he can be put off for soch a great person as the man I am now meeting at ze club! You vill gom ? "

" I should have been delighted—only unluckily I have a man dining with me. I tell you what! You come and join us! Will you? "

" If zat is ze only vay—yes, mit pleasure! Who is ze man? "

" Young Tulliwuddle. Do you remember going to a dance at Lord Tulliwuddle's, some five and a half years ago?"

" Himmel! Ha, ha! Veil do I remember! "

" Well, our host of that evening died the other day, and this fellow is his heir—a second or third cousin whose existence was so displeasing to the old peer that he left him absolutely nothing that wasn't entailed, and never said 'How-do-you-do?' to him in his life. In consequence, he may not entertain you as much as I should like."

" If he is your friend, I shall moch enjoy his society! "

" I am flattered, but hardly convinced. Tulliwuddle's intellect is scarcely of the sparkling kind. However, come and try."

The hour, the place, were arranged; a reminiscence or two exchanged; fresh suggestions thrown out for the rejuvenation of a Bavarian magnate; another baronial laugh shook the foundations of the club; and then, as the afternoon was wearing on, the Baron hailed a cab and galloped for Belgrave Square, and the late Mr. Bunker sauntered off along Pall Mall.

" Who can despair of human nature while the Baron von Blitzenberg adorns the earth? " he reflected. " The discovery of champagne and the invention of summer holidays were minor events compared with his descent from Olympus !"

He bought a button-hole at the street corner and cocked his hat> more airily than ever.

" A volcanic eruption may inspire one to succor humanity, a wedding to condole with it, and a general election to warn it of its folly; but the Baron inspires one to amuse ! "

Meanwhile that Heaven-sent nobleman, with a manner enshrouded in mystery, was comforting his wife.

" Ah, do not grieve, mine Alicia ! No doubt ze Duke vill be disappointed not to see us to-night, but I have telegraphed. Ja, I have said I had so important an

affair. Ach, do not veep! I did not know you wanted so moch to dine mit ze old Duke. I sopposed you vould like a quiet evening at home. But anyhow I have now telegraphed—and my leetle dinner mit my friend—Ach, it is so important zat I most rosh and get dressed. Cheer up, my loff! Good-by! "

He paused in answer to a tearful question.

" His name? Alas, I have promised not to say. You vould not have a European war by my indiscretion? "

CHAPTER III

WITH mirrors reflecting a myriad lights, with the hum of voices, the rustle of satin and lace, the hurrying steps of waiters, the bubbling of laughter, of life, and of wine—all these on each side of them, and a plate, a foaming glass, and a friend in front, the Baron and his host smiled radiantly down upon less favored mortals.

" Tulliwuddle is very late," said Essington; " but he's a devilish casual gentleman in all matters."

" I am selfish enoff to hope he vill not gom at all!" exclaimed the Baron.

" Unfortunately he has had the doubtful taste to conceive a curiously high opinion of myself. I am afraid he won't desert us. But I don't propose that we shall suffer for his slackness. Bring the fish, waiter."

The Baron was happy ; and that is to say that his laughter re-echoed from the shining mirrors, his tongue was loosed, his heart expanded, his glass seemed ever empty.

" Ach, how to make zis joie de vivre to last beyond tonight! " he cried. " May ze Teufel fly off mit offeecial duties and receptions and — and even mit my vife for a few days."

" My dear Baron! "

" To Alicia!" cried the Baron hastily, draining glass at the toast. " But some fun first! "

" * I could not love thee, dear, so well, Loved I not humor more!'"

his

misquoted his host gaily. "Ah!" he added, "here comes Tulliwuddle."

A young man, with his hands in his pockets and an eyeglass in his eye, strolled up to their table.

" I'm beastly sorry for being so late," said he; " but I'm hanged if I could make up my mind whether to risk wearing one of these frilled shirt-fronts. It's not bad, I think, with one's tie tied this way. What do you say?"

" It suits you like a halo," Essington assured him. " But let me introduce you to my friend the Baron Rudolph von Blitzenberg."

Lord Tulliwuddle bowed politely and took the empty chair; but it was evident that his attention could not concentrate itself upon sublunary matters till the shirt-front had been critically inspected and appreciatively praised by his host. Indeed, it was quite clear that Essington had not exaggerated his regard for himself. This admiration was perhaps the most pleasing feature to be noted on a brief acquaintance with his lordship. He was obviously intended neither for a strong man of action nor a great man of thought. A tolerable appearance and considerable amiability he might no doubt claim; but unfortunately the effort to retain his eyeglass had apparently the effect of forcing his mouth

chronically open, which somewhat marred his appearance; while his natural good-humor lapsed too frequently into the lamentations of an idle man that Providence neglected him or that his creditors were too attentive.

It happens, however, that it is rather his circumstances than his person which concern this history. And, briefly, these were something in this sort. Born a poor relation and guided by no strong hand, he had gradually seen himself, as Reverend uncles and Right Honorable cousins died off, approach nearer and nearer to the ancient barony of Tulliwuddle (created 1475 in the peerage of Scotland), until this year he had actually succeeded to it. But after his first delight in this piece of good fortune had subsided he began to realize in himself two notable deficiencies: very clearly, the lack of money, and more vaguely, the want of any preparation for filling the shoes of a stately courtier and famous Highland chieftain. He would often, and with considerable feeling, declare that any ordinary peer he could easily have become, but that being old Tulliwuddle's heir, by Gad! he didn't half like the job.

At present he was being tolerated or befriended by a small circle of acquaintances, and rapidly becoming a familiar figure to three or four tailors and half a dozen door-keepers at the stage entrances to divers Metropolitan theatres. In the circle of acquaintances, the humorous sagacity of Essington struck him as the most astonishing thing he had ever known. He felt, in fact, much like a village youth watching his first conjuring

performance, and while the whim lasted (a period which Essington put down as probably six weeks) he would have gone the length of paying a bill or ordering a tie on his recommendation alone.

To-night the distinguished appearance and genial conversation of Essington's friend impressed him more than ever with the advantages of knowing so remarkable a personage. A second bottle succeeded the first, and a third the second, the cordiality of the dinner growing all the while, till at last his lordship had laid aside the last traces of his national suspicion of even the most charming strangers.

" I say, Essington," he said, " I had meant to tell you about a devilish delicate dilemma I'm in. I want your advice."

" You have it," interrupted his host. " Give her a five-pound note, see that she burns your letters, and introduce her to another fellow."

" But—er—that wasn't the thing "

" Tell him you'll pay in six months, and order another pair of trousers," said Essington, briskly as ever.

" But, I say, it wasn't that "

"My dear Tulliwuddle, I never give racing tips."

"Hang it! "

"What is the matter?"

Tulliwuddle glanced at the Baron.

" I don't know whether the Baron would be interested "

"Immensely, my goot Tollyvoddle! Supremely! hugely! I could be interested to-night in a museum!"

"The Baron's past life makes him a peculiarly catholic judge of indiscretions," said Essington.

Thus reassured, Tulliwuddle began—

"You know I've an aunt who takes an interest in me— wants me to collar an heiress and that sort of thing. Well, she has more or less arranged a marriage for me."

"Fill your glasses, gentlemen!" cried Essington.

"Hoch, hoch!" roared the Baron.

"But, I say, wait a minute! That's only the beginning. I don't know the girl—and she doesn't know me."

He said the last words in a peculiarly significant tone.

"Do you wish me to introduce you?"

"Oh, hang it! Be serious, Essington. The point is—will she marry me if she does know me?"

"Himmel! Yes, certainly!" cried the Baron.

"Who is she?" asked their host, more seriously.

"Her father is Darius P. Maddison, the American Silver King."

The other two could not withhold an exclamation.

"He has only two children, a son and a daughter, and he wants to marry his daughter to an English peer—or a Scotch, it's all the same. My aunt knows 'em pretty well, and she has recommended me."

"An excellent selection," commented his host.

"But the trouble is, they want rather a high-ciass peer. Old Maddison is deuced particular, and I believe the girl is even worse."

"What are the qualifications desired?"

"Oh, he's got to be ambitious, and a promising young man—and elevated tastes—and all that kind of nonsense."

"But you can be all zat if you try!" said the Baron eagerly. "Go to Germany and get trained. I did vork twelve hours a day for ten years to be vat I am."

"I'm different," replied the young peer gloomily. "Nobody ever trained me. Old Tulliwuddle might have taken me up if he had liked, but he was prejudiced against me. I can't become all those things now."

"And yet you do want to marry the lady?"

"My dear Essington, I can't afford to lose such a chance! One doesn't get a Miss Maddison every day. She's a deuced handsome girl too, they say."

"By Gad, it's worth a trip across the Atlantic to try your luck," said Essington. "Get 'em to guarantee your expenses and you'll at least learn to play poker and see Niagara for nothing."

"They aren't in America. They've got a salmon river in Scotland, and they are there now. It's not far from my place, Hechnahoul."

"She's practically in your arms, then?"

"Ach. Ze affair is easy!"

"Pipe up the clan and abduct her!"

"Approach her mit a kilt!"

But even those optimistic exhortations left the peer still melancholy.

"It sounds all very well," said he, "but my clansmen, as you call 'em, would expect such a devil of a lot from me too. Old Tulliwuddle spoiled them for any ordinary mortal. He went about looking like an advertise-

ment for whisky, and called 'em all by their beastly Gaelic names. I have never been in Scotland in my life, and I can't do that sort of thing. I'd merely make a fool of myself. If I'd had to go to America it wouldn't have been so bad."

At this weak-kneed confession the Baron could hardly withhold an exclamation of contempt, but Essington, with more sympathy, inquired—

" What do you propose to do, then? "

His lordship emptied his glass.

" I wish I had your brains and your way of carrying things off, Essington! " he said, with a sigh. " If you got a chance of showing yourself off to Miss Mad-dison she'd jump at you! "

A gleam, inspired and humorous, leaped into Essing-ton's eyes. The Baron, whose glance happened at the moment to fall on him, bounded gleefully from his seat.

" Hoch! " he cried, " it is mine old Bonker zat I see before me! Vat have you in your mind? "

" Sit down, my dear Baron ; that lady over there thinks you are preparing to attack her. Shall we smoke? Try these cigars."

Throwing the Baron a shrewd glance to calm his somewhat alarming exhilaration, their host turned with a graver air to his other guest.

" Tulliwuddle," said he, " I should like to help you."

" I wish to the deuce you could ! "

Essington bent over the table confidentially.

" I have an idea."

CHAPTER IV

THE three heads bent forward towards a common centre—the Baron agog with suppressed • excitement, Tulliwuddle revived with curiosity and a gleam of hope, Essington impressive and cool.

"I take it," he began, "that if Mr. Darius P. Maddison and his coveted daughter could see a little of Lord Tulliwuddle—meet him at lunch, talk to him afterwards, for instance—and carry away a favorable impression of the nobleman, there would not be much difficulty in subsequently arranging a marriage? "

" Oh, none," said Tulliwuddle. " They'd be only too keen, if they approved of me; but that's the rub, you know."

" So far so good. Now it appears to me that our modest friend here somewhat underrates his own powers of fascination "

" Ach, Tollyvoddle, you do indeed," interjected the Baron.

" But since this idea is so firmly established in his mind that it may actually prevent him from displaying himself to the greatest advantage, and since he has been good enough to declare that he would regard with

complete confidence my own chances of success were I in his place, I would propose— with all becoming diffidence—that I should interview the lady and her parent instead of him."

" A vary vise idea, Bonker," observed the Baron.

"What!" said Tulliwuddle. "Do you mean that you would go and crack me up, and that sort of thing?"

" No; I mean that I should enjoy a temporary loan of your name and of your residence, and assure them by a personal inspection that I have a sufficient assortment of virtues for their requirements."

" Splendid! " shouted the Baron. " Tollyvoddle, accept zis generous offer before it is too late! "

" But," gasped the diffident nobleman, " they would find out the next time they saw me."

" If the business is properly arranged, that would only be when you came out of church with her. Look here —what fault have you to find with this scheme? I produce the desired impression, and either propose at once and am accepted "

" H'm," muttered Tulliwuddle doubtfully.

" Or I leave things in such good train that you can propose and get accepted afterwards by letter."

" That's better," said Tulliwuddle.

" Then, by a little exercise of our wits, you find an excuse for hurrying on the marriage— have it a private affair for family reasons, and so on. You will be prevented by one excuse or another from meeting the lady till the wedding-day. We shall choose a darkish church, you will have a plaster on your face—and the deed is done!"

" Not a fault can I find," commented the Baron sagely. " Essington, I congratulate you."

Between his complete confidence in Essington and the Baron's unqualified commendation, Lord Tulliwuddle was carried away by the project.

" I say, Essington, what a good fellow you are! " he cried. " You really think it will work ? "

" What do you say, Baron? "

" It cannot fail, I do solemnly . assure you. Be thankful you have soch a friend, Tollyvoddle! "

" You don't think anybody will suspect that you aren't really me? "

" Does any one up at Hechnahoul know you ? "

" No."

" And no one there knows me. They will never suspect for an instant."

His lordship assumed a look that would have been serious, almost impressive, had he first removed his eyeglass. Evidently some weighty consideration had occurred to him.

" You are an awfully clever chap, Essington," he said, " and deuced superior to most fellows, and—er—all that kind of thing. But—well—you don't mind my saying it?"

"My morals? My appearance? Say anything you like, my dear fellow."

" It's only this, that noblesse oblige, and that kind of thing, you know."

" I am afraid I don't quite follow."

" Well, I mean that you aren't a nobleman, and do you think you could carry things off like a—ah—like a Tulliwuddle? "

Essington remained entirely serious.

" I shall have at my elbow an adviser whose knowledge of the highest society in Europe is, without exaggeration, unequalled. Your perfectly natural doubts will be laid at rest when I tell you that I hope to be accompanied by the Baron Rudolph von Blitzen-berg."

The Baron could no longer contain himself.

" Himmel! Hurray! My dear friend, I vill go mit you to hell!"

" That's very good of you," said Essington, " but you mistake my present destination. I merely wish your company as far as the Castle of Hechnahoul."

" I gom mit so moch pleasure zat I cannot eggspress! Tollyvoddle, be no longer afraid. I have helped to write a book on ze noble families of Germany—zat is to say, I have contributed my portrait and some anecdote. Our dear friend shall make no mistakes! "

By this guarantee Lord Tulliwuddle's last doubts were completely set at rest. His spirits rose as he perceived how happily this easy avenue would lead him out of all his troubles. He insisted on calling for wine and pledging success to the adventure with the most resolute and confident air, and nothing but a few details remained now to be settled. These were chiefly with regard to the precise limits up to which the duplicate Lord Tulliwuddle might advance his conquering arms.

" You won't formally propose, will you ? " said the first edition of that peer.

" Certainly not, if you prefer to negotiate the surrender yourself," the later impression assured him.

" And you mustn't—well—er "

" I shall touch nothing."

"A girl might get carried away by you," said the original peer a trifle doubtfully.

" The Baron is the most scrupulous of men. He will be by my side almost continually. Baron, you will act as my judge, my censor, and my chaperon? "

" Tollyvoddle, I swear to you zat I shall use an eye like ze eagle. He shall be so careful—ach, I shall see to it! Myself, I am a Bayard mit ze ladies, and Bonker he shall not be less so! "

" Thanks, Baron, thanks awfully," said his lordship. " Now my mind is quite at rest!"

In the vestibule of the restaurant they bade goodnight to the confiding nobleman, and then turned to one another with an adventurer's smile.

:< You are sure you can leave your diplomatic duties?" asked Essington.

" Zey vill be my diplomatic duties zat I go to do! Oh, I shall prepare a leetle story—do not fear me."

The Baron chuckled, and then burst forth—

" Never was zere a man like you. Oh, cunning Mistair Bonker! And you vill give me zomezing to do in ze adventure, eh ? "

" I promise you that, Baron."

As he gave this reassuring pledge, a peculiar smile stole over Mr. Bunker's face—a smile that seemed to suggest even happier possibilities than either of his distinguished friends contemplated.

CHAPTER V

IT is at all times pleasant to contemplate thorough workmanship and sagacious foresight, particularly when these are allied with disinterested purpose and genuine enthusiasm. For the next few days Mr. Bunker, preparing to carry out to the best of his ability the delicate commission with which he had been entrusted, presented this stimulating spectacle.

Absolutely no pains were left untaken. By the aid of some volumes lent him by Tulliwuddle he learned, and digested in a pocketbook, as much information as he thought necessary to acquire concerning the history of the noble family he was temporarily about to enter; together with notes of their slogan or war-cry (spelled phonetically to avoid the possibility of a mistake), of their acreage, gross and net rentals, the names of their land-agents, and many other matters equally to the point. It was further to be observed that he spared no pains to imprint these particulars in the Baron's Teutonic memory—whether to support his own in case of need, or for some more secret purpose, it were impossible to fathom. Disguised as unconspicuous and harmless persons, they would meet in many quiet haunts whose unsuspected excellences they could guarantee from their old experience, and there mature their philanthropic plan.

Not only had its talented originator to impress the Tulliwuddle annals and statistics into his ally's eager mind, but he had to exercise the nicest tact and discernment lest the Baron's excess of zeal should trip their enterprise at the very outset.

" To-day I have told Alicia zat my visit to Russia vill probably be vollowed by a visit to ze Emperor of China," the Baron would recount with vast pride in his inventive powers. " And I have dropped a leetle hint zat for an envoy to be imprisoned in China is not to be surprised. Zat vill prepare her in case I am away longer zan ve expect."

" And how did she take that intimation? " asked Es-sington, with a less congratulatory air than he had expected.

" I did leave her in tears."

" My dear Baron, fly to her to tell her you are not going to China! She will get so devilish alarmed if you are gone a week that she'll go straight to the embassy and make inquiries."

He shook his head, and added in an impressive voice —

" Never lie for lying's sake, Blitzenberg. Besides, how do you propose to forge a Chinese post-mark? "

The Baron had laid the foundations of his Russian trip on a sound basis by requesting a friend of his in that country to post to the Baroness the bi-weekly budgets of Muscovite gossip which he intended to compose

at Hechnahoul. This, it seemed to him, would be a simple feat, particularly with his friend Bunker to assist; but he had to confess that the provision of Chinese news would certainly be more difficult.

" Ach, veil, I shall contradict China," he agreed.

It will be readily believed that what with getting up his brief, pruning the legends with which the Baron proposed to satisfy his wife and his ambassador, and purchasing an outfit suitable to the roles of peer and chieftain, this indefatigable gentleman passed three or four extremely busy days.

" Ve most start before my dear mozzer-in-law does gom!" the Baron more than once impressed upon him, so that there was no moment to be wasted.

Two days before their departure Mr. Bunker greeted his ally with a peculiarly humorous smile.

" The pleasures of our visit to Hechnahoul are to be considerably augmented," said he. " Tulliwuddle has only just made the discovery that his ancestral castle is let; but his tenant, in the most handsome spirit, invites us to be his guests so long as we are in Scotland. A very hospitable letter, isn't it? "

He handed him a large envelope with a more than proportionately large crest upon it, and drawing from this a sheet of note-paper headed by a second crest, the Baron read this epistle:

" MY LOUD, —Learning that you propose visiting your Scottish estates, and Mr. M'Fadyen, your factor, informing me no lodge is at present available for your

reception, it will give Mrs. Gallosh and myself great pleasure, and we will esteem it a distinguished honor, if you and your friend will be our guests at Hechnahoul Castle during the duration of your visit. Should you do us the honor of accepting, I shall send my steam launch to meet you at Torrydhulish pier and convey you across the loch, if you will be kind enough to advise me which train you are coming by.

" In conclusion, Mrs. Gallosh and myself beg to assure you that although you find strangers in your ancestral halls, you will receive both from your tenantry and ourselves a very hearty welcome to your native land. Believe me, your obedient servant,

"DUNCAN JNO. GALLOSH."

"Zat is goot news!" cried the Baron. "Ve shall have company—perhaps ladies! Ach, Bonker, I have ze soft spot in mine heart: I am so constant as ze needle to ze pole; but I do like sometimes to talk mit voman!"

"With Mrs. Gallosh, for instance?"

"But, Bonker, zere may be a Miss Gallosh."

"If you consulted the Baroness," said Bunker, smiling, "I suspect she would prefer you to be imprisoned in China."

The Baron laughed, and curled his martial mustache with a dangerous air.

"Who is zis Gallosh?" he inquired.

"Scottish, I judge from his name; commercial, from his literary style; elevated by his own exertions, from the size of his crest ; and wealthy, from the fact that he

COUNT BUNKER

rents Hechnahoul Castle. His mention of Mrs. Gallosh points to the fact that he is either married or would have us think so; and I should be inclined to conclude that he has probably begot a family."

"Aha!" said the Baron. "Ve vill gom and see, eh?"

CHAPTER VI

A CAREFULLY clothed young man, with an eyeglass and a wavering gait, walked slowly out of Euston Station. He had just seen the Scottish express depart, and this event seemed to have filled him with dubious reflections. In fact, at the very last moment Lord Tulliwuddle's confidence in his two friends had been a trifling degree disturbed. It occurred to him as he lingered by the door of their reserved first-class compartment that they had a little too much the air of gentlemen departing on their own pleasure rather than on his business. No sooner did he drop a fretful hint of this opinion than their affectionate protestations had quickly revived his spirit; but now that they were no longer with him to counsel and encourage, it once more drooped.

"Confound it!" he thought, "I hadn't bargained on having to keep out of people's way till they came back. If Essington had mentioned that sooner, I don't know that I'd have been so keen about the notion. Hang it! I'll have to chuck the Morrells' dance. And I can't go with the Greys to Ranelagh. I can't even dine with my own aunt on Sunday. Oh, the devil!"

The perturbed young peer waved his umbrella and climbed into a hansom.

COUNT BUNKER

"Well, anyhow, I can still go on seeing Connie. That's some consolation," he told himself; and without stopping to consider what would be the thoughts of his two obliging friends had they known he was seeking consolation in the society of one lady while they were arranging his nuptials with another, the baptismal Tulli-wuddle drove back to the civilization of St. James's.

Within the reserved compartment was no foreboding, no faint-hearted paling of the cheek. As the train clattered, hummed, and presently thundered on its way, the two laughed cheerfully towards one another, delighted beyond measure with the prosperous beginning of their enterprise. The Baron could not sufficiently express his gratitude and admiration for the promptitude with which his friend had purveyed so promising an adventure.

"Ve vill have f on, my Bonker. Ach! ve vill," he exclaimed for the third or fourth time within a dozen miles from Euston.

His Bunker assumed an air half affectionate, half apologetic.

" I only regret that I should have the lion's share of the adventure, my dear Baron."

" Yes," said the Baron, with a symptom of a sigh, " I do envy you indeed. Yet I should not say zat "

Bunker swiftly interrupted him.

" You would like to play a worthier part than merely his lordship's friend? "

"Ach! if I could."

Bunker smiled benignantly.

" Ah, Baron, you cannot suppose that I would really do Tulliwuddle such injustice as to attempt, in my own feeble manner, to impersonate him? "

The Baron stared.

"Vat mean you?"

" You shall be the lion, / the humble necessary jackal. As our friend so aptly quoted, noblesse oblige. Of course, there can be no doubt about it. You, Baron, must play the part of peer, I of friend."

The Baron gasped.

"Impossible!"

" Quite simple, my dear fellow."

" You—you don't mean so ? "

" I do indeed."

" Bot I shall not do it so veil as you."

" A hundred times better."

" Bot vy did you not say so before? "

" Tulliwuddle might not have agreed with me."

" Bot vould he like it now? "

" It is not what he likes that we should consider, it's what is good for his interests."

"Bot if I should fail?"

" He will be no worse off than before. Left to himself, he certainly won't marry the lady. You give him his only chance."

"Bot more zan you vould, really and truthfully?"

" My dear Baron, you are admitted by all to be an ideal German nobleman. Therefore you will certainly make an ideal British peer. You have the true Grand-Seigneur air. No one would mistake you for anything but a great aristocrat, if they merely saw you in bathing pants; whereas I have something a little different about my manner. I'm not so impressive—not so hall-marked, in fact."

His friend's omniscient air and candidly eloquent tone impressed the Baron considerably. His ingrained conviction of his own importance accorded admirably with these arguments. His thirst for " life " craved this lion's share. His sanguine spirit leaped at the appeal. Yet his well-regulated conscience could not but state one or two patent objections.

" Bot I have not read so moch of the Tollyvoddles as you. I do not know ze strings so veil."

" I have told you nearly everything I know. You will find the rest here."

Essington handed him the note-book containing his succinct digest. In intelligent anticipation of this contingency it was written in his clearest handwriting.

" You should have been a German," said the Baron admiringly.

He glanced with sparkling eyes at the note-book, and then with a distinctly greater effort the Teutonic conscience advanced another objection.

" Bot you have bought ze kilt, ze Highland hat, ze brogue shoes."

" I had them made to your measurements."

The Baron impetuously embraced his thoughtful friend. Then again his smile died away.

" Bot, Bonker, my voice! Zey tell me I haf nozing zat you vould call qvite an accent; bot a foreigner-one does regognize him, eh ? "

" I shall explain that in a sentence. The romantic tincture of—well, not quite accent, is a pleasant little piece of affectation adopted by the young bloods about the Court in compliment to the German connections of the Royal family."

The Baron raised no more objections.

" Bonker, I agree! Tollyvoddle I shall be, by Jove and all!"

He beamed his satisfaction, and then in an eager voice asked—

" You haf not ze kilt in zat hat-box? "

Unfortunately, however, the kilt was in the van.

Now the journey, propitiously begun, became more exhilarating, more exciting with each mile flung by. The Baron, egged on by his friend's high spirits and his own imagination to anticipate pleasure upon pleasure, watched with rapture the summer landscape whiz past the windows. Through the flat midlands of England they sped; field after field, hedgerow after hedgerow, trees by the dozen, by the hundred, by the thousand, spinning by in one continuous green vista. Red brick towns, sluggish rivers, thatched villages and ancient churches dark with yews, the shining web of junctions, and a whisking glimpse of wayside stations leaped towards them, past them, and leagues away behind. But swiftly as they sped, it was all too slowly for the fresh-created Lord Tulliwuddle.

"Are we not nearly to Scotland yet?" he inquired some fifty times.

" * My heart's in the Highlands a-chasing the

COUNT BUNKER

dears!'" hummed the abdicated nobleman, whose hilarity had actually increased (if that were possible) since his descent into the herd again.

All the travellers' familiar landmarks were hailed by the gleeful diplomatist with encouraging comments.

" Ach, look! Beauteef ul view! How quickly it is gone! Hurray! Ve must be nearly to Scotland."

A panegyric on the rough sky-line of the north country fells was interrupted by the entrance of the dining-car attendant. Learning that they would dine, he politely inquired in what names he should engage their seats. Then, for an instant, a horrible confusion nearly overcame the Baron. He—a von Blitzenberg— to give a false name! His color rose, he stammered, and only in the nick of time caught his companion's eye.

" Ze Lord Tollyvoddle," he announced, with an effort as heroic as any of his ancestors' most warlike enterprises.

Too impressed to inquire how this remarkable title should be spelled, the man turned to the other distinguished-looking passenger.

" Bunker," said that gentleman, with smiling assurance.

The man went out.

" Now are ve named!" cried the Baron, his courage rising the higher for the shock it had sustained. " And you vunce more vill be Bonker ? Goot! "

"That satisfies you?"

The Baron hesitated.

" My dear friend, I have a splendid idea! Do you know I did disgover zere used to be a nobleman in Austria really called Count Bonker? He vas a famous man; you need not be ashamed to take his name. Vy should not you be Count Bonker ? "

" You prefer to travel in titled company ? Well, be hanged—why not! When one comes to think of it, it seems a pity that my sins should always be attributed to the middle classes."

Accordingly this history has now the honorable task of chronicling the exploits of no fewer than two noblemen.

LATE that evening they reached a city which the home-coming chieftain in an outburst of Celtic fervor dubbed " mine own bonny Edinburg!" and there they repaired for the night to a hotel. Once more the Baron (we may still style him so since the peerage of Tulliwuddle was of that standing also) showed a certain diffidence when it came to answering to his new title in public; but in the seclusion of their private sitting-room he was careful to assure his friend that this did not arise from any lack of nerve or qualms of conscience, but merely through a species of headache—the result of railway travelling.

" Do not fear for me," he declared as he stirred the sugar in his glass, " I have ze heart of a lion."

The liquid he was sipping being nothing less potent than a brew of whisky punch, which he had ordered (or rather requested Bunker to order) as the most romantically national compound he could think of, produced, indeed, a fervor of foolhardiness. He insisted upon opening the door wide, and getting Bunker to address him as " Tollyvoddle," in a strident voice, " so zat zey all may hear," and then answering in a firm " Yes, Count Bonker, vat vould you say to me? "

46

It is true that he instantly closed the door again, and even bolted it, but his display seemed to make a vast impression upon himself.

" Many men vould not dare so to go mit anozzer name," he announced; " bot I have my nerves onder a good gontrol."

" You astonish me," said the Count.

"I do even surprise myself," admitted the Baron.

In truth the ordeal of carelessly carrying off an alias is said by those who have undergone it (and the report is confirmed by an experienced class of public officials) to require a species of hardihood which, fortunately for society, is somewhat rare. The most daring Smith will sometimes stammer when it comes to merely answering " Yes " to a cry of " Brown!" and Count Bunker, whose knowledge of human nature was profound and remarkably accurate, was careful to fortify his friend by example and praise, till by the time they went to bed the Baron could scarcely be withheld from seeking out the manager and airing his assurance upon him. Or, at least, he declared he would have done this had he been sure that the manager was not already in bed himself.

Unfortunately at this juncture the Count committed one of those indiscretions to which a gay spirit is always prone, but which, to do him justice, seldom sullied his own record as a successful adventurer. At an hour considerably past midnight, hearing an excited summons from the Baron's bedroom, he laid down his toothbrush and hastened across the passage, to

find the new peer in a crimson dressing-gown of quilted silk gazing enthusiastically at a lithograph that hung upon the wall.

" See!" he cried gleefully, " here is my own ancestor. Bonker, I feel I am Tollyvoddle indeed."

The print which had inspired this enthusiasm depicted a historical but treasonable Lord Tulliwuddle preparing to have his head removed.

Giving it a droll look, the Count observed—

" Well, if it inspires you, my dear Baron, that's all right. The omen would have struck me differently."

" Ze omen! " murmured the Baron with a start.

It required all Bunker's tact to revive his ally's damped enthusiasm, and even at breakfast next morning he referred in a gloomy voice to various premonitions recorded in the history of his family, and the horrible consequences of disregarding them.

But by the time they had started upon their journey north, his spirits rose a trifle; and when at length all lowland landscapes were left far behind them, and they had come into a province of peat streams and granite pinnacles, with the gloom of pines and the freshness of the birch blended like a May and December marriage, all appearance, at least, of disquietude had passed away.

Yet the Count kept an anxious eye upon him. He was becoming decidedly restless. At one moment he would rave about the glorious scenery; the next, plunge into a brown study of the Tulliwuddle rent-roll; and then in an instant start humming an air and

smoking so fast that both their cases were empty while they were yet half an hour from Torrydhulish Station. Now the Baron took to biting his nails, looking at his watch, and answering questions at random—a very different spectacle from the enthusiastic traveller of yesterday.

" Only ten minutes more," observed Bunker in his most cheering manner.

The Baron made no reply.

They were now running along the brink of a glimmering loch, the piled mountains on the farther shore perfectly mirrored; a tern or two lazily fishing; a delicate summer sky smiling above. All at once Count Bunker started—

" That must be Hechnahoul! " said he.

The Baron looked and beheld, upon an eminence across the loch, the towers and turrets of an imposing mansion overtopping a green grove.

" And here is the station," added the Count.

The Baron's face assumed a piteous expression.

" Bonker," he stammered, " I —I am afraid! You be ze Tollyvoddle— I cannot do him! "

" My dear Baron ! "

"Oh, I cannot!"

" Be brave — for the honor of the fatherland. Play the bold Blitzenberg ! "

" Ach, ja; but not bold Tolly voddle. Zat picture— you vere right — it vas omen! "

Never did the genius of Bunker rise more audaciously to an occasion.

COUNT BUNKER

" My dear Baron," said he, assuming on the instant a confidence-inspiring smile, " that print was a hoax; it wasn't old Tulliwuddle at all. I faked it myself."

"So?" gasped the Baron. "You assure me truly?"

Muttering (the historian sincerely hopes) a petition for forgiveness, Bunker firmly answered—

" I do assure you! "

The train had stopped, and as they were the only first-class passengers on board, a peculiarly magnificent footman already had his hand upon the door. Before turning the handle, he touched his hat.

" Lord Tulliwuddle ? " he respectfully inquired.

" Ja—z&t is, yes, I am," replied the Baron.

CHAPTER VIII

FROM the platform down to the pier was only some fifty yards, and before them the travellers perceived an exceedingly smart steam-launch, and a stout middle-aged gentleman, in a blue serge suit and yachting cap, advancing from it to greet them. They had only time to observe that he had a sanguine complexion, iron-gray whiskers, and a wide-open eye, before he raised the cap and, in a decidedly North British accent, thus addressed them—

" My lord—ahem!—your lordship, I should say— I presume I've the pleasure of seeing Lord Tulli-wuddle?"

The Count gently pushed his more distinguished friend in front. With an embarrassment equal to their host's, his lordship bowed and gave his hand.

" I am ze Tollyvoddle —vary pleased—Mistair Gosh, I soppose? "

" Gallosh, my lord. Very honored to welcome you."

In the round eyes of Mr. Gallosh, Count Bunker perceived an unmistakable stare of astonishment at the sound of his lordship's accented voice. The Baron, on his part, was evidently still suffering from his attack of stage fright; but again the Count's gifts smoothed the creases from the situation.

" You have not introduced me to our host, Tulli-wuddle," he said, with a gay, infectious confidence.

" Ah, so! Zis is my friend Count Bunker—gom all ze vay from Austria," responded the Baron, with no glimmer of his customary aplomb.

Making a mental resolution to warn his ally never to say one word more about his fictitious past than was wrung by cross-examination, the distinguished-looking Austrian shook his host's hand warmly.

" From Austria via London," he explained in his pleasantest manner. " I object altogether to be considered a foreigner, Mr. Gallosh; and, in fact, I often tell Tulliwuddle that people will think me more English than himself. The German fashions so much in vogue at Court are transforming the very speech of your nobility. Don't you sometimes notice it?"

Thus directly appealed to, Mr. Gallosh became manifestly perplexed.

" Yes—yes, you're right in a way," he pronounced cautiously. " I suppose they do that. But will ye not take a seat? This is my launch. Hi! Robert, give his lordship a hand on board!"

Two mariners and a second tall footman assisted the guests to embark, and presently they were cutting the waters of the loch at a merry pace.

In the prow, like youth, the Baron insisted upon sitting with folded arms and a gloomy aspect; and as his nerve was so patently disturbed, the Count decidedly approved of an arrangement which left his host and himself alone together in the stern. In his present state of mind the Baron was capable of any indiscretion were he compelled to talk; while, silent and brooding in isolated majesty, he looked to perfection the part of returning exile. So, evidently, thought Mr. Gallosh.

" His lordship is looking verra well," he confided to the Count in a respectfully lowered voice.

" The improvement has been remarkable ever since his foot touched his native heath."

" You don't say so," said Mr. Gallosh, with even greater interest. " Was he delicate before ? "

" A London life, Mr. Gallosh."

" True — true, he'll have been busy seeing his friends; it'll have been verra wearing."

" The anxiety, the business of being invested, and so on, has upset him a trifle. You must put down any little—well, peculiarity to that, Mr. Gallosh."

" I understand—aye, umh'm, quite so. He'll like to be left to himself, perhaps ? "

" That depends on his condition," said the Count diplomatically.

" It's a great responsibility for a young man; yon's a big property to look after," observed Mr. Gallosh in a moment.

" You have touched the spot!" said the Count warmly. " That is, in fact, the chief cause of Tulli-wuddle's curious moodiness ever since he succeeded to the title. He feels his responsibilities a little too acutely."

Again Mr. Gallosh ruminated, while his guest from the corner of his eye surveyed him shrewdly.

" My forecast was wonderfully accurate," he said to himself.

The silence was first broken by Mr. Gallosh. As if thinking aloud, he remarked—

" I was awful surprised to hear him speak! It's the Court fashion, you say?"

" Partly that; partly a prolonged residence on the Continent in his youth. He acquired his accent then; he has retained it for fashion's sake," explained the Count, who thought it as well to bolster up the weakest part of his case a little more securely.

With this prudent purpose, he added, with a flattering air of taking his host into his aristocratic confidence—

" You will perhaps be good enough to explain this to the friends and dependants Lord Tulliwuddle is about to meet? A breath of unsympathetic criticism would grieve him greatly if it came to his ears."

"Quite, quite," said Mr. Gallosh eagerly. "I'll make it all right. I understand the sentiment pair-fectly. It's verra natural—verra natural indeed."

At that moment the Baron started from his reverie with an affrighted air.

" Vat is zat strange sound! " he exclaimed.

The others listened.

" That's just the pipes, my lord," said Mr. Gallosh. " They're tuning up to welcome you."

His lordship stared at the shore ahead of them.

" Zere are many peoples on ze coast!" he cried. "Vat makes it for?"

" They've come to receive you," his host explained. " It's just a little spontaneous demonstration, my lord."

His lordship's composure in no way increased.

" It was Mrs. Gallosh organized a wee bit entertainment on his lordship's landing," their host explained confidentially to the Count. " It's just informal, ye understand. She's been instructing some of the tenants—and ma own girls will be there—but, oh, it's nothing to speak of. If he says a few words in reply, that'll be all they'll be expecting."

The strains of " Tulliwuddle wha hae" grew ever louder and, to an untrained ear, more terrific. In a moment they were mingled with a clapping of hands and a Highland cheer, the launch glided alongside the pier, and, supported on his faithful friend's arm, the panic-stricken Tulliwuddle staggered ashore. Before his dazed eyes there seemed to be arrayed the vastest and most barbaric concourse his worst nightmare had ever imagined. Six pipers played within ten paces of him, each of them arrayed in the full panoply of the clan; at least a dozen dogs yelped their exulta- ; tion; and from the surrounding throng two ancient men in tartan and four visions in snowy white stepped forth to greet the distinguished visitors.

The first hitch in the proceedings occurred at this point. According to the unofficial but carefully considered programme, the pipers ought to have ceased their melody; but, whether inspired by ecstatic loyalty or because the Tulliwuddle pibroch took longer to perform than had been anticipated, they continued to skirl with such vigor that expostulations passed entirely unheard. Under the circumstances there was nothing for it but shouting, and in a stentorian yell Mr. Gallosh introduced his wife and three fair daughters.

Thereupon Mrs. Gallosh, a broad-beamed matron whose complexion contrasted pleasantly with her costume, delivered the following oration—

" Lord Tulliwuddle, in the name of the women of Hechnahoul—I may say in the name of the women of all the Highlands—oor ain Heelands, my lord " (this with the most insinuating smile)—" I bid you welcome to your ancestral estates. Remembering the conquests your ancestors used to make both in war and in a gentler sphere" (Mrs. Gallosh looked archness itself), " we ladies, I suppose, should regard your homecoming with some misgivings; but, my lord, every bonny Prince Charlie has his bonny Flora Macdonald, and in this land of mountain, mist, and flood, where ' Dark Ben More frowns o'er the wave,' and where ' Ilka lassie has her laddie,' you will find a thousand romantic maidens ready to welcome you as Ellen welcomed Fitz-James! For centuries your heroic race has adorned the halls and trod the heather of Hechnahoul, and for centuries more we hope to see the offspring of your lordship and some winsome Celtic maid rule these cataracts and glens! "

At this point the exertion of shouting down six bagpipes in active eruption caused a temporary cessation of the lady's eloquence, and the pause was filled by the cheers of the crowd led by the " Hip-hip-hip!" of Count Bunker, and by the broken and fortunately inaudible protests of the embarrassed father of future Tulliwuddles. In a moment Mrs. Gallosh had resumed—

" Lord Tulliwuddle, though I myself am only a stranger to your clan, your Highland heart will feel reassured when I mention that I belong through my grandmother to the kindred clan of the Mackays!" ("Hear, hear!" from two or three ladies and gentlemen, evidently guests of the Gallosh.) " We are but visitors at Hechnahoul, yet we assure you that no more devoted hearts beat in all Caledonia! Lord Tulliwuddle, we welcome you! "

" Put your hand on your heart and bow," whispered Bunker. " Keep on bowing and say nothing! "

Mechanically the bewildered Baron obeyed, and for a few moments presented a spectacle not unlike royalty in procession.

But as some reply from him had evidently been expected at this point, and the pipers had even ceased playing lest any word of their chief's should be lost, a pause ensued which might have grown embarrassing had not the Count promptly stepped forward.

" I think," he said, indicating two other snow-white figures who held gigantic bouquets, " that a pleasant part of the ceremony still remains before us."

With a grateful glance at this discerning guest,
COUNT BUNKER
Mrs. Gallosh thereupon led forward her two youngest daughters (aged fifteen and thirteen), who, with an air so delightfully coy that it fell like a ray of sunshine on the poor Baron's heart, presented him with their flowery symbols of HechnahouFs obeisance to its lord.

His consternation returned with the advance of the two ancient clansmen who, after a guttural panegyric in Gaelic, offered him further symbols—a claymore and target, very formidable to behold. All these gifts having been adroitly transferred to the arms of the footmen by the ubiquitous Count, the Baron's emotions swiftly passed through another phase when the eldest Miss Gallosh, aged twenty, with burning eyes and the most distracting tresses, dropped him a sweeping courtesy and offered a final contribution—a fiery cross, carved and painted by her own fair hands.

A fresh round of applause followed this, and then a sudden silence fell upon the assembly. All eyes were turned upon the chieftain: not even a dog barked: it was the moment of a lifetime.

" Can you manage a speech, old man ? " whispered Bunker.

" Ach, no, no, no! Let me escape. Oh, let me fly! "

" Bury your face in your hands and lean on my shoulder," prompted the Count.

This stage direction being obeyed, the most effective tableau conceivable was presented, and the climax was reached when the Count, after a brief dumb-show intended to indicate how vain were Lord Tulliwuddle's efforts to master his emotion, spoke these words in the most thrilling accents he could muster—

" Fair ladies and brave men of Hechnahoul! Your chief, your friend, your father requests me to express to you the sentiments which his over-wrought emotions prevent him from uttering himself. On his behalf I tender to his kind and courteous friends, Mr., Mrs., and the fair maids Gallosh, the thanks of a long-absent exile returned to his native land for the welcome they have given him! To his devoted clan he not only gives his thanks, but his promise that all rents shall be reduced by one half—so long as he dwells among them ! " (Tumultuous applause, disturbed only by a violent ejaculation from a large man in knickerbockers whom Bunker justly judged to be the factor.)

" With his last breath he shall perpetually thunder: Ahasheen—comara—mohr! "

The Tulliwuddle slogan, pronounced with the most conscientious accuracy of which a Sassenach was capable, proved as effective a curtain as he had anticipated; and amid a perfect babel of cheering and bagpiping the chieftain was led to his host's carriage.

CHAPTER IX

WELL, the worst of it is over," said Bunker cheerfully. The Baron groaned. " Ze vorst is only jost beginning to gommence."

They were sitting over a crackling fire of logs in the sitting-room of the suite which their host had reserved for his honored visitors. How many heirlooms and dusky portraits the romantic thoughtfulness of the ladies had managed to crowd into this apartment for the occasion were hard to compute; enough, certainly, one would think, to inspire the most sluggish-blooded Tulliwuddle with a martial exultation. Instead, the chieftain groaned again.

" Tell zem I am ill. I cannot gom to dinner. Tomorrow I shall take ze train back to London. Himmel ! Vy vas I fool enoff to act soch dishonorable lies! I deceive all these kind peoples! "

" It isn't that which worries me," said Bunker im-perturbably. " I am only afraid that if you display this spirit you won't deceive them."

" I do not vish to," said the Baron sulkily.

It required half an hour of the Count's most artful bkndishments to persuade him that duty, honor, and prudence all summoned him to the feast. This being accomplished, he next endeavored to convince him that he would feel more comfortable in the airy freedom of the Tulliwuddle tartan. But here the Baron was obdurate. Now that the kilt lay ready to his hand he could not be persuaded even to look at it. In gloomy silence he donned his conventional evening dress and announced, last thing before they left their room—

" Bonker, say no more! To-morrow morning I depart!"

Their hostess had explained that a merely informal dinner awaited them, since his lordship (she observed) would no doubt prefer a quiet evening after his long journey. But Mrs. Gallosh was one of those good ladies who are fond of asking their friends to take " pot luck," and then providing them with fourteen courses; or suggesting a " quiet little evening together," when they have previously removed the drawing-room carpet. It is an affectation of modesty apt to disconcert the retiring guest who takes them at their word. In the drawing-room of Mrs. Gallosh the startled Baron found assembled—firstly, the Gallosh family, consisting of all those whose acquaintance we have already made, and in addition two stalwart schoolboy sons; secondly, their house-party, who comprised a Mr. and Mrs. Rentoul, from the same metropolis of commerce as Mr. Gallosh, and a hatchet-faced young man with glasses, answering to the name of Mr. Cromarty-Gow; and, finally, one or two neighbors. These last included Mr. M'Fadyen, the large factor; the

Established Church, U.F., Wee Free, Episcopalian, and Original Secession ministers, all of whom, together with their kirks, flourished within a four-mile radius of the Castle; the wives to three of the above; three young men and their tutor, being some portion of a reading-party in the village; and Mrs. Cameron-Campbell and her five daughters, from a neighboring dower-house upon the loch.

It was fortunate that all these people were prepared to be impressed with Lord Tulliwuddle, whatever he should say or do; and further, that the unique position of such a famous hereditary magnate even led them to anticipate some marked deviation from the ordinary canons of conduct. Otherwise, the gloomy brows; the stare, apparently haughty, in reality alarmed; the strange accent and the brief responses of the chief guest, might have caused an unfavorable opinion of his character.

As it was, his aloofness, however natural, would probably have proved depressing had it not been for the gay charm and agreeable condescension of the other nobleman. Seldom had more rested upon that adventurer's shoulders, and never had he acquitted himself with greater credit. It was with considerable secret concern that he found himself placed at the opposite end of the table from his friend, but his tongue rattled as gaily and his smiles came as readily as ever. With Mrs. Cameron-Campbell on one side, and a minister's lady upon the other, his host two places distant, and a considerable audience of silent eaters within earshot, he successfully managed to divert the attention of quite half the table from the chieftain's moody humor.

" I always feel at home with a Scotsman," he discoursed genially. " His imagination is so quick, his intellect so clear, his honesty so remarkable, and" (with an irresistible glance at the minister's lady) " his wife 'so charming."

" Ha, ha! " laughed Mr. Gallosh, who was mellowing rapidly under the influence of his own champagne. " I'm verra glad to see you know good folks when you meet them. What do you think now of the English? "

Having previously assured himself that his audience was neat Scotch, the polished Austrian unblushingly replied—

" The Englishman, I have observed, has a slightly slower imagination, a denser intelligence, and is less conspicuous for perfect honesty. His womankind also have less of that nameless grace and ethereal beauty which distinguish their Scottish sisters."

It is needless to say that a more popular visitor never was seen than this discriminating foreigner, and if his ambitions had not risen above a merely personal triumph, he would have been in the highest state of satisfaction. But with a disinterested eye he every now and then sought the farther end of the table, where, between his hostess and her charming eldest daughter, and facing his factor, the Baron had to endure his ordeal unsupported.

" I wonder how the devil he's getting on!" he more than once said to himself.

For better or for worse, as the dinner advanced, he began to hear the Court accent more frequently, till his curiosity became extreme.

" His lordship seems in better spirits," remarked Mr. Gallosh.

" I hope to Heaven he may be!" was the fervent thought of Count Bunker.

At that moment the point was settled. With his old roar of exuberant gusto the Baron announced, in a voice that drowned even the five ministers—

" Ach, yes, I vill toss ze caber to-morrow! I vill toss him—-so high!" (his napkin flapped upwards). " How long shall he be ? So tall as my castle I Mees Gallosh, you shall help me? Ach, yes! Mit hands so fair ze caber vill spring like zis!"

His pudding-spoon, in vivid illustration, skipped across the table and struck his factor smartly on the shirt-front.

" Sare, I beg your pardon," he beamed with a graciousness that charmed Mrs. Gallosh even more than his spirited conversation—" Ach, do not return it, please! It is from my castle silver—keep it in memory of zis happy night! "

The royal generosity of this act almost reconciled Mrs. Gallosh to the loss of one of her own silver spoons.

" Saved! " sighed Bunker, draining his glass with a relish he had not felt in any item of the feast hitherto.

Now that the Baron's courage had returned, .no heraldic lion ever pranced more bravely. His laughter, his jests, his compliments were showered upon the delighted diners. Mr. Gallosh and he drank healths down the whole length of the table " mit no tap-heels! " at least four times. He peeled an orange for Miss Gallosh, and cut the skin into the most diverting figures, pressing her hand tenderly as he presented her with these works of art. He inquired of Mrs. Gallosh the names of the clergymen, and, shouting something distantly resembling these, toasted them each and all with what he conceived to be appropriate comments. Finally he rose to his feet, and, to the surprise and delight of all, delivered the speech they had been disappointed of earlier in the day.

" Goot Mr. Gallosh, fair Mrs. Gallosh, divine Mees Gallosh, and all ze ladies and gentlemans, how sorry I vas I could not make my speech before, I cannot eggspress. I had a headache, and vas not veil vithin. Ach, soch zings vill happen in a new climate. Bot now I am inspired to tell you I loff you all! I zank you eggstremely! How can I return zis hospitality? I vill tell you! You must all go to Bavaria and stay mit "

" Tulliwuddle! Tulliwuddle! " shouted Bunker frantically, to the great amazement of the company. " Allow me to invite the company myself to stay with me in Bavaria ! "

The Baron turned crimson, as he realized the abyss of error into which he had so nearly plunged. Adroitly
COUNT BUNKER
the Count covered his confusion with a fit of laughter so ingeniously hearty that in a

moment he had joined in it too.

" Ha, ha, ha! " he shouted. " Zat was a leetle joke at my friend's eggspense. It is here, in my castle, you shall visit me; some day very soon I shall live in him. Meanvile, dear Mrs. Gallosh, gonsider it your home! For me you make it heaven, and I cannot ask more zan zat! Now let us gom and have some f on! "

A salvo of applause greeted this conclusion. At the Baron's impetuous request the cigars were brought into the hall, and ladies and gentlemen all trooped out together.

" I cannot vait till I have seen Miss Gallosh dance ze Highland reel," he explained to her gratified mother; " she has promised me."

" But you must dance too, Lord Tulliwuddle," said ravishing Miss Gallosh. " You know you said you would."

" A promise to a lady is a law," replied the Baron gallantly, adding in a lower tone, " especially to so fair a lady! "

"It's a pity his lordship hadn't on his kilt," put in Mr. Gallosh genially.

"By ze Gad, I vill put him on! Hoch! Ve vill have some f on! "

The Baron rushed from the hall, followed in a moment by his noble friend. Bunker found him already wrapping many yards of tartan about his waist.

" But, my dear fellow, you must take off your trousers," he expostulated.

Despite his glee, the Baron answered with something of the Blitzenberg dignity—

" Ze bare leg I cannot show to-night—not to dance mit ze young ladies. Ven I have practised, perhaps; but not now, Bonker."

Accordingly the portraits of four centuries of Tulli-wuddles beheld their representative appear in the very castle of Hechnahoul with his trouser-legs capering beneath an ill-hung petticoat of tartan. And, to make matters worse in their canvas eyes, his own shameless laugh rang loudest in the mirth that greeted his entrance.

" Ze garb of Gaul!" he announced, shaking with hilarity. " Gom, Bonker, dance mit me ze Highland fling!"

The first night of Lord Tulliwuddle's visit to his ancestral halls is still remembered among his native hills. The Count also, his mind now rapturously at ease, performed prodigies. They danced together what they were pleased to call the latest thing in London, sang a duet, waltzed with the younger ladies, till hardly a head was left unturned, and, in short, sent away the ministers and their ladies, the five Miss Cameron-Campbells, the reading-party, and particularly the factor, with a new conception of a Highland chief. As for the house-party, they felt that they were fortunate beyond the lot of most ordinary mortals.

CHAPTER X

THE Baron sat among his heirlooms, laboriously disengaging himself from his kilt. Fitfully throughout this process he would warble snatches of an air which Miss Gallosh had sung.

" Whae vould not dee for Sharlie? " he trolled, " Ze yong chevalier!"

" Then you don't think of leaving to-morrow morn-ning? " asked Count Bunker, who was watching him with a complacent air.

" Mein Gott, no fears! "

"We had better wait, perhaps, till the afternoon? "

" I go not for tree veeks! Gaben sie—das ist, gim'me zat tombler. Vun more of mountain juice to ze health of all Galloshes 1 Partic'ly of vun! Eh, old Bonker?"

The Count took care to see that the mountain juice was well diluted. His friend had already found Scottish hospitality difficult to enjoy in moderation.

"Baron, you gave us a marvellously lifelike representation of a Jacobite chieftain!"

The Baron laughed a trifle vacantly.

"Ach, it is easy for me. Himmel, a Blitzenberg should know how! Vollytoddle—Toddyvolly—whatsh my name, Bonker?"

The Count informed him.

"Tollivoddlesh is nozing to vat I am at home! Ab-s'lutely nozing! I have a house twice as big as zis, and servants—Ach, so many I know not! Bot, mein Bonker, it is not soch fon as zis! Mein Gott, I most get to bed. I toss ze caber to-morrow."

And upon the arm of his faithful ally he moved cautiously towards his bedroom.

But if he had enjoyed his evening well, his pleasure was nothing to the gratification of his hosts. They could not bring themselves to break up their party for the night: there were so many delightful reminiscences to discuss.

"Of all the evenings ever I spent," declared Mr. Gallosh, "this fair takes the cake. Just to think of that aristocratic young fellow being as companionable-like! When first I put eyes on him, I said to myself— * You're not for the likes of us. All lords and ladies is your kind. Never a word did he say in the boat till he heard the pipes play, and then I really thought he was frightened! It must just have been a kind of home-sickness or something."

"It'll have been the tuning up that set his teeth on edge," Mrs. Gallosh suggested practically.

"Or perhaps his heart was stirred with thoughts of the past!" said Miss Gallosh, her eyes brightening.

In any case, all were agreed that the development of his hereditary instincts had been extraordinarily rapid.

"I never really properly talked with a lord before," sighed Mrs. Rentoul; "I hope they're all like this one."

'0

COUNT BUNKER

Mrs. Gallosh, on the other hand, who boasted of having had one tete-a-tete and joined in several general conversations with the peerage, appraised Lord Tulli-wuddle with greater discrimination.

"Ah, he's got a soupgon!" she declared. "That's what I admire!"

"Do you mean his German accent?" asked Mr. Cromarty-Gow, who was renowned for a cynical wit, and had been seeking an occasion to air it ever since Lord Tulliwuddle had made Miss Gallosh promise to dance a reel with him.

But the feeling of the party was so strongly against a breath of irreverent criticism, and their protest so emphatic, that he presently strolled off to the smoking-room, wishing that Miss Gallosh, at least, would exercise more critical discrimination.

"Do you think would they like breakfast in their own room, Duncan?" asked Mrs. Gallosh.

"Offer it them—offer it them; they can but refuse, and it's a kind of compliment to give them the opportunity."

"His lordship will not be wanting to rise early," said Mr. Rentoul. "Did you notice what an amount he could drink, Duncan? Man, and he carried it fine! But he'll be the better of a sleep-in in the morning, him coming from a journey too."

Mr. Rentoul was a recognized authority on such questions, having, before the days of his affluence, travelled for a notable firm of distillers. His praise of Lord Tulliwuddle's capacity was loudly echoed by Mr.

Gallosh, and even the ladies could not but indulgently agree that he had exhibited a strength of head worthy of his race.

" And yet he was a wee thing touched too," said Mr. Rentoul sagely. " Maybe you were too far gone yourself, Duncan, to notice it, and the ladies would just think it was gallantry; but I saw it in his voice and his legs—oh, just a wee thingie, nothing to speak of."

" Surely you are mistaken!" cried Miss Gallosh. " Wasn't it only excitement at finding himself at Hechnahoul? "

" There's two kinds of excitement," answered the oracle. " And this was the kind I'm best acquaint with. Oh, but it was just a wee bittie."

" And who thinks the worse of him for it ? " cried Mr. Gallosh.

This question was answered by general acclamation in a manner and with a spirit that proved how deeply his lordship's gracious behavior had laid hold of all hearts.

BREAKFAST in the private parlor was laid for two; but it was only Count Bunker, arrayed in a becoming suit of knickerbockers, and looking as fresh as if he had feasted last night on aerated water, who sat down to consume it.

" Who would be his ordinary everyday self when there are fifty more amusing parts to play," he reflected gaily, as he sipped his coffee. " Blitzenberg and Essington were two conventional members of society, ageing ingloriously, tamely approaching five-and-thirty in bath-chairs. Tulliwuddle and Bunker are paladins of romance! We thought we had grown up—thank Heaven, we were deceived! "

Having breakfasted and lit a cigarette, he essayed for the second time to arouse the Baron; but getting nothing but the most somnolent responses, he set out for a stroll, visiting the gardens, stables, kennels, and keeper's house, and even inspecting a likely pool or two upon the river, and making in the course of it several useful acquaintances among the Tulliwuddle retainers.

When he returned he found the Baron stirring a cup of strong tea and staring at an ancestral portrait with a thoughtful frown.

"They are preparing the caber, Baron," he remarked genially.

" Stoff and nonsense; I vill not fling her!" was the wholly unexpected reply. " I do not love to play ze fool alvays!"

" My dear Baron! "

" Zat picture," said the Baron, nodding his head solemnly towards the portrait. " It is like ze Lord Tol-lyvoddle in ze print at ze hotel. I do believe he is ze same."

" But I explained that he wasn't Tulliwuddle."

" He is so like," repeated the Baron moodily. " He most be ze same."

Bunker looked at it and shook his head.

" A different man, I assure you."

" Oh, ze devil! " replied the Baron.

"What's the matter?"

" I haff a head zat tvists and turns like my head never did since many years."

The Count had already surmised as much.

" Hang it out of the window," he suggested.

The Baron made no reply for some minutes. Then with an earnest air he began—

" Bonker, I have somezing to say to you."

" You have the most sympathetic audience outside the clan."

The Count's cheerful tone did not seem to please his friend.

" Your heart, he is too light, Bonker; ja, too light. Last night you did engourage me not to be seemly."

" I! "

" I did get almost dronk. If my head vas not so

COUNT BUNKER

hard I should be dronk. Das ist not right. If I am to be ze Tollyvoddle, it most be as I vould be Von Blitzenberg. I most not forget zat I am not as ozzer men. I am noble, and most be so accordingly."

" What steps do you propose to take ? " inquired Bunker with perfect gravity.

The Baron stared at the picture.

" Last night I had a dream. It vas zat man—at least, probably it vas, for I cannot remember eggs-actly. He did pursue me mit a kilt."

" With what did you defend yourself? "

"I know not: I jost remember zat it should be a warning. Ve Blitzenbergs have ze gift to dream."

The Baron rose from the table and lit a cigar. After three puffs he threw it from him.

" I cannot smoke," he said dismally. " It has a onpleasant taste."

The Count assumed a seriously thoughtful air.

" No doubt you will wish to see Miss Maddison as soon as possible and get it over," he began. " I have just learned that their place is about seven miles away. We could borrow a trap this afternoon "

" Nein, nein! " interrupted the Baron. " Donner-wetter! Ach, no, it most not be so soon. I most practise a leetle first. Not so immediately, Bon-ker."

Bunker looked at him with a glance of unfathomable calm.

" I find that it will be necessary for you to observe one or two ancient ceremonies, associated from time

immemorial with the accession of a Tulliwuddle. You are prepared for the ordeal? "

" I most do my duty, Bonker."

" This suggests some more inspiring vision than the gentleman in the gold frame," thought the Count acutely.

Aloud he remarked—

" You have high ideals, Baron."

" I hope so."

Again the Baron was the unconscious object of a humorous, perspicacious scrutiny.

" Last night I did hear zat moch was to be expected from me," he observed at length.

"From Mrs. Gallosh? "

" I do not zink it vas from Mrs. Gallosh."

Count Bunker smiled.

" You inflamed all hearts last night," said he.

The Baron looked grave.

" I did drink too moch last night. But I did not say vat I should not, eh? I vas not rude or gross to— Mistair Gallosh?"

" Not to Mr. Gallosh."

The Baron looked a trifle perturbed at the gravity of his tone.

" I vas not too free, too undignified in presence of zat innocent and charming lady—Miss Gallosh? "

The air of scrutiny passed from Count Bunker's face, and a droll smile came instead.

" Baron, I understand your ideals and I appreciate your motives. As you suggest, you had better rehearse

COUNT BUNKER

your part quietly for a few days. Miss Maddison will find you the more perfect suitor."

The Baron looked as though he knew not whether to feel satisfied or not.

" By the way," said the Count in a moment, " have you written to the Baroness yet? Pardon me for reminding you, but you must remember that your letters will have to go out to Russia and back."

The Baron started.

" Teufel! " he exclaimed. " I most indeed write."

" The post goes at twelve."

The Baron reflected gloomily, and then slowly moved to the writing-table and toyed with his pen. A few minutes passed, and then in a fretful voice he asked—

"Vat shall I say?"

" Tell her about your journey across Europe—how the crops look in Russia—what^you think of St. Petersburg—that sort of thing."

A silent quarter of an hour went by, and then the Baron burst out—

" Ach, I cannot write to-day! I cannot invent like you. Ze crops—I have got zat—and zat I arrived safe —and zat Petersburg is nice. Vat else? '*

" Anything you can remember from text-books on Muscovy or illustrated interviews with the Czar. Just a word or two, don't you know, to show you've been there; with a few comments of your own."

"Vat like comments?"

" Such as—' Somewhat annoyed with bombs this afternoon,' or * This caused me to reflect upon the dis-

advantages of an alcoholic marine'—any little bit of philosophy that occurs to you."

The Baron pondered.

" It is a pity zat I have not been in Rossia," he observed.

" On the other hand, it is a blessing your wife hasn't. Look at the bright side of things, my dear fellow."

For a short time, from the way in which the Baron took hasty notes in pencil and elaborated them in ink (according to the system of Professor Virchausen), it appeared that he was following his friend's directions. Later, from a sentimental look in his eye, the Count surmised that he was composing an amorous" addendum; and at last he laid down his pen with a sigh which the cynical (but only the cynical) might have attributed to relief.

" Ha, my head he is getting more clear! " he announced. " Gom, let us present ourselves to ze ladies, mine Bonker! "

CHAPTER XII

IT is necessary, Bonker—you are sure? " " No Tulliwuddle has ever omitted the ceremony. If you shirked, I am assured on the very best authority that it would excite the gravest suspicions of your authenticity."

Count Bunker spoke with an air of the most resolute conviction. Ever since they arrived he had taken infinite pains to discover precisely what was expected of the chieftain, and having by great good luck made the acquaintance of an elderly individual who claimed to be the piper of the clan, and who proved a perfect granary of legends, he was able to supply complete information on every point of importance. Once the Baron had endeavored to corroborate these particulars by interviewing the piper himself, but they had found so much difficulty in understanding one another's dialects that he had been content to trust implicitly to his friend's information. The Count, indeed, had rather avoided than sought advice on the subject, and the piper, after several confidential conversations and the passage of a sum of silver into his sporran, displayed an equally Delphic tendency.

The Baron, therefore, argued the present point no longer.

" It is jost a mere ceremony," he said. " Ach, veil, nozing vill happen. Zis ghost—vat is his name? "

"It is known as the Wraith of the Tulliwuddles. The heir must interview it within a week of coming to the Castle."

" Vere most I see him ? "

" In the armory, at midnight. You bring one friend, one candle, and wear a bonnet with one eagle's feather in it. You enter at eleven and wait for an hour—and, by the way, neither of you must speak above a whisper."

" Pooh! Jost hombog! " said the Baron valiantly. " I do not fear soch trash."

" When the Wraith appears "

" My goot Bonker, he vill not gom! "

" Supposing he does come—and mind you, strange things happen in these old buildings, particularly in the Highlands, and after dinner; if he comes, Baron, you must ask him three questions."

The Baron laughed scornfully.

" If I see a ghost I vill ask him many interesting questions—if he does feel cold, and sochlike, eh? Ha, ha!"

With an imperturbable gravity that was not without its effect upon the other, however gaily he might talk, Bunker continued —

"The three questions are: first, * What art thou?' second, * Why comest thou here, O spirit ?' third, ' What instructions desirest thou to give me ? ' Strictly speaking, they ought to be asked in Gaelic, but excep-

tions have been made on former occasions, and Mac-Dui—who pipes, by the way, in the anteroom—assures me that English will satisfy the Wraith in your

case.

The Baron sniffed and laughed, and twirled up the ends of his mustaches till they presented a particularly desperate appearance. Yet there was a faint intonation of anxiety in his voice as he inquired—

" You vill gom as my friend, of course ? "

" I? Quite out of the question, I am sorry to say. To bring a foreigner (as I am supposed to be) would rouse the clan to rebellion. No, Baron, you have a chance of paying a graceful compliment to your host which you must not lose. Ask Mr. Gallosh to share your vigil."

" Gallosh—he vould not be moch good sopposing

Ach, but nozing vill happen! I vill ask him."

The pride of Mr. Gallosh on being selected as his lordship's friend on this historic occasion was pleasant to witness.

"It's just a bit of fiddle-de-dee," he informed his delighted family. "Duncan Gallosh to be looking for bogles is pretty ridiculous—but oh, I can't refuse to disoblige his lordship."

"I should think not, when he's done you the honor to invite you out of all his friends!" said Mrs. Gallosh warmly. "Eva! do you hear the compliment that's been paid your papa?"

Eva, their fair eldest daughter, came into the room at a run. She had indeed heard (since the news was

on every tongue), and impetuously she flung her arms about her father's neck.

"Oh, papa, do him credit!" she cried; "it's like a story come true! What a romantic thing to happen!"

"What a spirit!" her mother reflected proudly. "She is just the girl for a chieftain's bride!"

That very night was chosen for the ceremony, and eleven o'clock found them all assembled breathless in the drawing-room: all, save Lord Tulliwuddle and his host.

"Will they have to wait for a whole hour?" asked Mrs. Gallosh in a low voice.

Indeed they all spoke in subdued accents.

"I am told," replied the Count, "that the apparition never appears till after midnight has struck. Any time between twelve and one he may be expected."

"Think of the terrible suspense after twelve has passed!" whispered Eva.

The Count had thought of this.

"I advised Duncan to take his flask," said Mr. Rentoul, with a solemn wink. "So he'll not be so badly off."

"Papa would never do such a thing to-night!" cried Eva.

"It's always a kind of precaution," said the sage.

Presently Count Bunker, who had been imparting the most terrific particulars of former interviews with the Wraith to the younger Galloshes, remarked that he must pass the time by overtaking some pressing correspondence.

"You will forgive me, I hope, for shutting myself up for an hour or so," he said to his hostess. "I shall come back in time to learn the results of the meeting."

And with the loss of his encouraging company a greater uneasiness fell upon the party.

Meanwhile, in a vast cavern of darkness, lit only by the solitary candle, the Baron and his host endeavored to maintain the sceptical buoyancy with which they had set forth upon their adventure. But the chilliness of the room (they had no fire, and it was a misty night with a moaning wind), the inordinate quantity of odd-looking shadows, and the profound silence, were immediately destructive to buoyancy and ultimately trying to scepticism.

"I wish ze piper vould play," whispered the Baron.

"Mebbe he'll begin nearer the time," his companion suggested.

The Baron shivered. For the first time he had been persuaded to wear the full panoply of a Highland chief, and though he had exhibited himself to the ladies with much pride, and even in the course of dinner had promised Eva Gallosh that he would never again don anything less romantic, he now began to think that a travelling-rug of the Tulliwuddle tartan would prove a useful addition to the outfit on the occasion of a midnight vigil. Also the stern prohibition against talking aloud (corroborated by the piper with many guttural warnings) gr v ew more and more irksome as the night advanced.

"It's an awesome place," whispered Mr. Gallosh.

"I hardly thought it would have been as lonesome-like."

There was a tremor in his voice that irritated the Baron.

"Pooh!" he answered, "it is jost vun old piece of hombog! I do not believe in soch things myself."

" Neither do I, my lord; oh, neither do I; but— would you fancy a dram? "

" Not for me, I zank you," said his lordship stiffly.

Blessing the foresight of Mr. Rentoul, his host unscrewed his flask and had a generous swig. As he was screwing on the top again, the Baron, in a less haughty voice, whispered—

" Perhaps" jost vun leetle taste."

They felt now for a few minutes more aggressively disposed.

" Ve need not have ze curtain shut," said the Baron. " Soppose you do draw him? "

Through the gloom Mr. Gallosh took one or two faltering steps.

" Man, it's awful hard to see one's way," he said nervously.

The Baron took the candle, and with a martial stride escorted him to the window. They pulled aside one corner of the heavy curtain, and then let it fall again and hurried back. So far north there was indeed a gleam of daylight left, but it was such a pale and ghostly ray, and the wreaths of mist swept so eerily and silently across the pane, that candle-light and shadows seemed vastly preferable.

COUNT BUNKER

"How much more time will there be?" whispered Mr. Gallosh presently.

" It is twenty-five minutes to twelve."

" Your lordship! Can we leave at twelve ? "

The Baron started.

" Oh, Himmel! " he exclaimed. " Vy did I not realize before? If nozing comes—and nozing vill come—ve most stay till one, I soppose."

Mr. Gallosh emitted something like a groan.

" Oh my, and that candle will not last more than half an hour at the most!"

"Teufel!" said the Baron. "It vas Bonker did give him to me. He might have made a more proper calculation."

The prospect was now gloomy indeed. An hour of candle-light had been bad, but an hour of pitch darkness or of mist wreaths would be many times worse.

"A wee tastie more, my lord?" Mr. Gallosh suggested, in a voice whose vibrations he made an effort to conceal.

" Jost a vee," said his lordship, hardly more firmly.

With a dismal disregard for their suspense the minutes dragged infinitely slowly. The flask was finished; the candle guttered and flickered ominously; the very shadows grew restless.

" There's a lot of secret doors and such like in this part of the house—let's hope there'll be nothing coming through one of them," said Mr. Gallosh in a breaking voice.

The Baron muttered an inaudible reply, and then with a start their shoulders bumped together.

" Damn it, what's yon! " whispered Mr. Gallosh.

" Ze pipes! Gallosh, how beastly he does play! "

In point of fact the air seemed to consist of only one wailing note.

" Bong! " —they heard the first stroke of midnight on the big clock on the Castle Tower; and so unfortunately had Count Bunker timed the candle that on the instant its flame expired.

" Vithdraw ze curtains! " gasped the Baron.

" I canna, my lord! Oh, I canna! " wailed Mr. Gallosh, breaking out into his broadest native Scotch.

This time 'the Baron made no movement, and in the palpitating silence the two sat through one long dark minute after another, till some ten of them had passed.

" I shall stand it no more!" muttered the Baron. " Ve vill creep for ze door."

" My lord, my lord! For maircy's sake gie's a hold of you! " stammered Mr. Gallosh, falling on his hands and knees and feeling for the skirt of his lordship's kilt.

But their flight was arrested by a portent so remarkable that had there been only a single witness one would suppose it to be a figment of his imagination. Fortunately, however, both the Baron and Mr. Gallosh can corroborate each detail. About the middle, apparently, of the wall opposite, an oblong of light appeared in the thickest of the gloom.

" Mein Gott! " cried the Baron.

COUNT BUNKER

"It's filled wi' reek!" gasped Mr. Gallosh.

And indeed the space seemed filled with a slowly rising cloud of pungent blue smoke. Then their horrified eyes beheld the figure of an undoubted Being hazily outlined behind the cloud, and at the same time the piper, as if sympathetically aware of the crisis, burst into his most dreadful discords. A yell rang through the gloom, followed by the sounds of a heavy body alternately scuffling across the floor and falling prostrate over unseen furniture. The Baron felt for his host, and realized that this was the escaping Gallosh.

" Tulliwuddle! Speak! " a hollow voice muttered out of the smoke.

The Baron has never ceased to exult over the hardihood he displayed in this unnerving crisis. Rising to his feet and drawing his claymore, he actually managed to stammer out—

" Who—who are you ? "

The Being (he could now perceive dimly that it was clad in tartan) answered in the same deep, measured voice—

" Your senses to confound and fuddle, Behold the Wraith of Tulliwuddle ! "

This was sufficiently terrifying, one would think, to excuse the Baron for following the example of his host. But, though he found afterwards that he must have perspired freely, he courageously stood his ground.

" Vy have you gomed here ? " he demanded in a voice nearly as hollow as the Wraith'

As solemnly as before the spirit replied—

" From Pit that's bottomless and dark— Methinks I hear it shrieking—Hark ! "

(The Baron certainly did hear a tumult that might well be termed infernal; though whether it emanated from Mr. Gallosh, fiends, or the piper, he could not at the moment feel certain.)

" I came o'er many leagues of heather To carry back the answer whether The noble chieftain of my clan Conducts him like a gentleman."

After this warning, to put the third question required an effort of the most supreme resolution. The Baron was equal to it, however.

" Vat instroction do you give me ? " he managed to utter.

In the gravest accents the Wraith chanted—

" Hang ever kilt above the knee, With Usquebaugh be not too free, When toasts and sic'like games be mooted See that your dram be well diluted; And oh, if you'd escape from Hades, Lord Tulliwuddle, 'ware the ladies ! "

The spirit vanished as magically as he had appeared, and with this solemn warning ringing in his ears, the Baron found himself in inky darkness again. This time he did not hesitate to grope madly for the door, but hardly had he reached it, when, with a fresh sensation of horror, he stumbled upon a writhing form that seemed to be pawing the panels. He was, fortunately; as quickly reassured by hearing the voice of Mr. Gal-losh exclaim in terrified accents—

" I canna find the haundle! Oh, Gosh, where's the haundle?"

Being the less frenzied of the two, the Baron did succeed in finding the handle, and with a gasp of relief burst into the lighted anteroom. The piper had already departed, and evidently in haste, since he had left some portion of a bottle of whisky unfinished. This fortunate circumstance enabled them to recover something of their color, though, even when he felt his blood warming again, Mr. Gallosh could scarcely speak coherently of his terrible ordeal.

" What an awfu' night! what an awfu' night! " he murmured. " Oh, my lord, let's get out of this! "

He was making for the door when the Baron seized his arm.

" Vait! " he cried. " Ze danger is past! Ach, vas I not brave? Did you not hear me speak to him? You can bear vitness how brave I vas, eh? "

" I'll not swear I heard just exactly what passed, my lord. Man, I'll own I was awful feared! "

" Tuts! tuts! " said the Baron kindly. " Ve vill say nozing about zat. You stood veil by me, I shall say. And you vill tell zem I did speak mit courage to ze ghost."

" I will that! " said Mr. Gallosh.

By the time they reached the drawing-room he had so far recovered his equanimity as to prove a very creditable witness, and between them they gave such an account of their adventure as satisfied even the excited expectations of their friends; though the Baron thought it both prudent and more becoming his dignity to leave considerable mystery attaching to the precise revelations of his ancestral spirit.

" Bot vere is Bonker?" he asked, suddenly noticing the absence of his friend.

A moment later the Count entered and listened with the greatest interest to a second (and even more graphic) account of the adventure. More intimate particulars still were confided to him when they had retired to their own room, and he appeared as surprised and impressed as any wraith-seer could desire. As they parted for the night, the Baron started and sniffed at him.

" Vat a strange smell you have!" he exclaimed.

" Peat smoke, probably. This fire wouldn't draw."

" Strange! " mused the Baron. " I did smell a leetle smell of zat before to-night."

" Yes ; one notices it all through the house with an east wind."

This seemed to the Baron a complete explanation of the coincidence.

CHAPTER XIII

AT the house in Belgrave Square at present tenanted by the Baron and Baroness von Blitzenberg, an event of considerable importance had occurred. This was nothing less than the arrival of the Countess of Grillyer upon a visit both of affection and state. So important was she, and so great the attachment of her daughter, that the preparations for her reception would have served for a reigning sovereign. But the Countess had an eye as quick and an appetite for respect as exacting as Queen Elizabeth, and she had no sooner embraced the Baroness and kissed her ceremoniously upon either cheek, than her glance appeared to seek something that she deemed should have been there also.

"And where is Rudolph?" she demanded. "Is he so very busy that he cannot spare a moment even to welcome me? "

The Baroness changed color, but with as easy an air as she could assume she answered that Rudolph had most unfortunately been summoned from England.

"Indeed?" observed the Countess, and the observation was made in a tone that suggested the advisability of a satisfactory explanation.

This paragon among mothers and peeresses was a lady of majestic port, whose ascendant expression and commanding voice were commonly held to typify all that is best in the feudal system; or, in other words, to indicate that her opinions had never been contradicted in her life. When one of these is a firm belief in the holder's divine rights and semi-divine origin, the effect is undoubtedly impressive. And the Countess impressed.

66 My dear Alicia," said she, when they had settled down to tea and confidential talk, " you "have not yet told me what has taken Rudolph abroad again so soon."

On nothing had the Baron laid more stress than on the necessity of maintaining the most profound secrecy respecting his mission. " No, not even to your mozzer most you say. My love, you vill remember? " had been almost his very last words before departing for St. Petersburg. His devoted wife had promised this not once, but many times, while his finger was being shaken at her, and would have scorned herself had she thought it possible to break her vows.

" That is a secret, mamma," she declared.

Her mother opened her eyes.

" A secret from me, Alicia ? "

" Rudolph made me promise."

" Not to tell your friends—but that hardly was intended to include your mother."

The Baroness looked uncomfortable.

" I — I'm afraid " she began, and stopped in hesitation.

" Did he specifically include me ? " demanded the Countess in an altered tone.

" I think, mamma, he did," her daughter faltered.

"Ah!"

And there was a world of meaning in that comment.

" Believe me, mamma, it is something very, very important, or Rudolph would certainly have let me tell you all about it."

Lady Grillyer opened her eyes still wider.

" Then I am to understand that he wishes to conceal from me anything that he considers of importance? "

" Oh, no! Not that! I only mean that this thing is very secret."

" Alicia," pronounced the Countess, " when a man specifically conceals anything from his mother-in-law, you may be quite certain that she ought to be informed of it at once."

" I—I can't, mamma! "

" A trip to Germany—for it is there, I presume, he has gone—back to the scenes of his bachelorhood, unprotected by the influence of his wife! Do you call that a becoming procedure? "

" But he hasn't gone to Germany."

" He has no business anywhere else! "

" You forget his diplomatic duties."

" Ah! He professes to have gone on diplomatic business ? "

" Professes, mamma? " exclaimed the poor Baroness. " How can you say such a thing! He certainly has gone on a diplomatic mission ! "

" To Paris, no doubt ? " suggested Lady Grillyer, with an intonation that made it quite impossible not to contradict her.

" Certainly not! He has gone to Russia."

The more the Countess learned, the more anxious she appeared to grow.

" To Russia, on a diplomatic mission ? This is incredible, Alicia! "

" Why should it be incredible ? " demanded Alicia, flushing.

" Because he is a mere tyro in diplomacy. Because there is a German embassy at Petersburg, and they would not send a man from London on a mission—at least, it is most unlikely."

" It seems to me quite natural," declared the Baroness.

She was showing more fight than her mother had ever encountered from her before, and the opposition seemed to inflame Lady Grillyer's resentment against the unfilial couple.

" You know nothing about it! What is this mission about?"

" That certainly is a secret," said Alicia, relieved that there was something left to keep her promise over.

" Has he gone alone ? "

" I—I mustn't tell you, mamma."

Alicia's face betrayed this subterfuge.

" You do not know yourself, Alicia," said the Countess incisively. " And so you need no longer pretend to be keeping a secret from me. It now becomes our joint business to discover the actual truth. Do not attempt to wrangle with me further! This investigation is necessary for your peace of mind, dear."

The unfortunate Baroness dropped a silent tear.. Her peace of mind had been serenely undisturbed till this moment, and now it was only broken by the thought of her husband's displeasure should he ever learn how she had disobeyed his injunctions. Further investigation was the very last thing to cure it, she said to herself bitterly. She looked piteously at her parent, but there she only saw an expression of concentrated purpose.

" Have you any reason, Alicia, to suspect an attachment—an affair of any kind? "

"Mamma!"

" Do not jump in that excitable manner. Think quietly. He has evidently returned to Germany for some purpose which he wishes to conceal from us: the natural supposition is that a woman is at the bottom of it."

" Rudolph is incapable "

" No man is incapable who is in the full possession of his faculties. I know them perfectly."

" But, mamma, I cannot bear to think of such a thing!"

" That is a merely middle-class prejudice. I can't imagine where you have picked it up."

In point of fact, during Alicia's girlhood Lady Grill-yer had always been at the greatest pains to preserve her daughter's innocent simplicity, as being preemi-

nently a more marketable commodity than precocious worldliness. But if reminded of this she would probably have retorted that consistency was middle-class also.

"I have no reason to suspect anything of the sort," the Baroness declared emphatically.

Her mother indulged her with a pitying smile and inquired—

"What other explanation can you offer? Among his men friends is there anyone likely to lead him into mischief?"

"None—at least "

"Ah!"

"He promised me he would avoid Mr. Bunker—I mean Mr. Essington."

The Countess started. She had vivid and exceedingly distasteful recollections of Mr. Bunker.

"That man! Are they still acquainted?"

"Acquainted—oh yes; but I give Rudolph credit for more sense and more truthfulness than to renew their friendship."

The Countess pondered with a very grave expression upon her face, while Alicia gently wiped her eyes and ardently wished that her honest Rudolph was here to defend his character and refute these baseless insinuations. At length her mother said with a brisker air—

"Ah! I know exactly what we must do. I shall make a point of seeing Sir Justin Wallingford tomorrow."

"Sir Justin Wallingford!"

"If anybody can obtain private information for us he can. We shall soon learn whether the Baron has been sent to Russia."

Alicia uttered a cry of protest. Sir Justin, ex-diplomatist, author of a heavy volume of Victorian reminiscences, and confidant of many public personages, was one of her mother's oldest friends; but to her he was only one degree less formidable than the Countess, and quite the last person she would have chosen for consultation upon this, or indeed upon any other subject.

"I am not going to intrust my husband's secrets to him!" she exclaimed.

"I am," replied the Countess.

"But I won't allow it! Rudolph would be "

"Rudolph has only himself to blame. My dear Alicia, you can trust Sir Justin implicitly. When my child's happiness is at stake I would consult no one who was not discretion itself. I am very glad I thought of him."

The Baroness burst into tears.

"My child, my child!" said her mother compassionately. "The world is no Garden of Eden, however much we may all try to make it so."

"You—you don't se—seem to be trying now, mamma."

"May Heaven forgive you, my darling," pronounced the Countess piously.

CHAPTER XIV

SIR JUSTIN," said the Countess firmly, " please tell my daughter exactly what you have discovered."

Sir Justin Wallingford sat in the drawing-room at Belgrave Square with one of these ladies on either side of him. He was a tall, gaunt man with a grizzled black beard, a long nose, and such a formidably solemn expression that ambitious parents were in the habit of wishing that their offspring might some day be as wise as Sir Justin Wallingford looked. His fund of information was prodigious, while his reasoning powers were so remarkable that he had never been known to commit the slightest action without furnishing a full and adequate explanation of his conduct. Thus the discrimination shown by the Countess in choosing him to restore a lady's peace of mind will at once be apparent.

" The results of my inquiries," he pronounced, " have been on the whole of a negative nature. If this mission on which the Baron von Blitzenberg professes to be employed is in fact of an unusually delicate nature, it is just conceivable that the answer I received from Prince Gommell-Kinchen, when I sounded him at the Khalifa's luncheon, may have been intended merely

COUNT BUNKER

to throw dust in my eyes. At the same time, his highness appeared to speak with the candor of a man who has partaken, not excessively, you understand, but I may say freely, of the pleasures of the table."

He looked steadily first at one lady and then at the other, to let this point sink in.

" And what did the Prince say ? " asked the Baroness, who, in spite of her supreme confidence in her husband, showed a certain eager nervousness inseparable from a judicial inquiry.

" He told me—I merely give you his word, and not my own opinion; you perfectly understand that, Baroness ? "

" Oh yes," she answered hurriedly.

" He informed me that, in fact, the Baron had been obliged to ask for a fortnight's leave of absence to attend to some very pressing and private business in connection with his Silesian estates."

" I think, Alicia, we may take that as final," said her mother decisively.

"Indeed / shan't!" cried Alicia warmly. "That was just an excuse, of course. Rudolph's business is so very delicate that—that—well, that you could only expect Prince Gommell-Kinchen to say something of that sort."

"What do you say to that, Sir Justin?" demanded the Countess.

With the air of a man doing what was only his duty, he replied—

" I say that I think it is improbable. In fact, since

you demand to know the truth, I may inform you that the Prince added that leave of absence was readily given, since the Baron's diplomatic duties are merely nominal. To quote his own words, ' Von Blitzenberg is a nice fellow, and it pleases the English ladies to play with him."

Even Lady Grillyer was a trifle taken aback at this description of her son-in-law, while Alicia turned scarlet with anger.

" I don't believe he said anything of the sort!" she cried. " You both of you only want to hurt me and insult Rudolph! I won't stand it! "

She was already on her feet to leave them, when her mother stopped her, and Sir Justin hastened to explain.

" No reflection upon the Baron's character was intended, I assure you. The Prince merely meant to imply that he represented the social rather than the business side of the embassy. And both are equally necessary, I assure you—equally essential, Baroness, believe me."

" In fact," said the Countess, " the remark comes to this, that Rudolph would never be sent to Russia, whatever else they might expect of him."

Even through their tears Alicia's eyes brightened with triumph.

" But he has gone, mamma! I got a letter from him this morning — from St. Petersburg! "

The satisfaction of her two physicians on hearing this piece of good news took the form of a start which

COUNT BUNKER

might well have been mistaken for mere astonishment, or even for dismay.

" And you did not tell me of it!" cried her mother.

" Rudolph did not wish me to. I have only told you now to prove how utterly wrong you both are."

" Let me see this letter! "

" Indeed, mamma, I won't! "

The two ladies looked at one another with such animosity that Sir Justin felt called upon to interfere.

" Suppose the Baroness were to read us as much as is necessary to convince us that there is no possibility of a mistake," he suggested.

So profoundly did the Countess respect his advice that she graciously waived her maternal rights so far as actually following the text with her eyes went; while her daughter, after a little demur, was induced to depart this one step further from her husband's injunctions.

" You have no objections to my glancing at the post-mark?" said Sir Justin when this point was settled.

With a toss of her head the Baroness silently handed him the envelope.

" It seems correct," he observed cautiously.

" But post-marks can be forged, can't they ? " inquired the Countess.

" I fear they can," he admitted, with a sorrowful air.

Scorning to answer this insinuation, the Baroness proceeded to read aloud the following extracts—

" ' I travelled with comfort through Europe, and having by many countries passed, such as Germany and others, I arrived, my dear Alicia, in Russia.' "

" Is that all he says about his journey? " interrupted Lady Grillyer.

" It is certainly a curiously insufficient description of a particularly interesting route," commented Sir Justin.

" It almost seems as if he didn't know what other countries lie between England and Russia," added the Countess.

" It only means that he knows geography doesn't interest me! " replied Alicia. " And he does say more about his journey—'Alone by myself, in a carriage very quietly I travelled.' And again—* To be observed not wishing, and strict orders being given to me, with no man I spoke all the way.' There!"

" That certainly makes it more difficult to check his statements," Sir Justin admitted.

" Ah, he evidently thought of that! " said the Countess. " If he had said there was anyone with him, we could have asked him afterwards who it was. What a pity! Read on, my child—we are vastly interested."

Thus encouraged, the Baroness continued—

" * In Russia the crops are good, and from my window with pleasure I observe them. Petersburg is a nice town, and I have a pleasant apartment in it!' :

" What! " exclaimed the Countess. " He is looking at the crops from his window in St. Petersburg!"

Sir Justin grimly pursed his lips, but his silence was

more ominous than speech. In fact, the Baron's unfortunate effort at realism by the introduction of his window struck the first blow at his wife's implicit trust in him. She was evidently a little disconcerted, though she stoutly declared—

" He is evidently living in the suburbs, mamma."

" Will you be so kind as to read on a little farther? " interposed Sir Justin in a grave voice.

" ' The following reflections have I made. Russia is very large and cold, where people in furs are to be seen, and sledges. Bombs are thrown sometimes, and the marine is not good when it does drink too much.' Now, mamma, he must have seen these things or he wouldn't put them in his letter."

The Baroness broke off somewhat hurriedly to make this comment, almost indeed as though she felt it to be necessary. As for her two comforters, they looked at one another with so much sorrow that their eyes gleamed and their lips appeared to smile.

" The Baron did not write that letter in Russia," said Sir Justin decisively. " Furs are not worn in summer, nor do the inhabitants travel in sledges at this time of the year."

" But—but he doesn't say he actually saw them," pleaded the Baroness.

" Then that remark, just like the rest of his reflections, makes utter nonsense," rejoined her mother.

" Is that all? " inquired Sir Justin.

"Almost all—all that is important," faltered the Baroness.

" Let us hear the rest," said her mother inexorably.

" There is only a postscript, and that merely says— ' The flask that you filled I thank you for; it was so

large that it was sufficient for ' I can't read the

last word."

" Let me see it, Alicia."

A few minutes ago Alicia would have torn the precious letter up rather than let another eye fall upon it. That her devotion was a little disturbed was proved by her allowing her two advisers to study even a single sentence. Keeping her hand over the rest, she showed it to them. They bent their brows, and then simultaneously exclaimed—

" < Us both! ' "

" Oh, it can't be!" cried the poor Baroness.

" It is absolutely certain," said her mother in a terrible voice— " * It was so large that it was sufficient for us both!'"

" There is no doubt about it," corroborated Sir Justin sternly. " The unfortunate young man has inadvertently confessed his deception."

" It cannot be! " murmured the Baroness. " He said at the beginning that he travelled quite alone."

" That is precisely what condemns him," said her mother.

" Precisely," reiterated Sir Justin.

The Baroness audibly sobbed, while the two patchers of her peace of mind gazed at her commiserately.

" What am I to do? " she asked at length. " I can't believe he really But how am I to find out? "

COUNT BUNKER

" I shall make further investigations," promptly replied Sir Justin.

" And I also," added the Countess.

" Meanwhile," said Sir Justin, " we shall be exceedingly interested to learn what further particulars of his wanderings the Baron supplies you with."

" Yes," observed the Countess, " he can fortunately be trusted to betray himself. You will inform me, Alicia, as soon as you hear from him again."

Her daughter made no reply.

Sir Justin rose and bade them a grave farewell.

" In my daughter's name I thank you cordially," said the Countess, as she pressed his hand.

" Anything I have done has been a pleasure to me," he assured them with a sincerity there was no mistaking.

CHAPTER XV

IN an ancient and delightful garden, where glimpses of the loch below gleamed through a mass of summer foliage, and the gray castle walls looked down on smooth, green glades, the Baron slowly paced the shaven turf. But he did not pace it quite alone, for by his side moved a graceful figure in a wide, sun-shading hat and a frock entirely irresistible. Beneath the hat, by bending a little down, you could have seen the dark liquid eyes and tender lips of Eva Gallosh. And the Baron frequently bent down.

" I am proud of everyzing zat I find in my home," said the Baron gallantly.

The lady's color rose, but not apparently in anger.

" Ach, here is a pretty leetle seat!" he exclaimed in a tone of pleased discovery, just as though he had not been leading her insidiously towards it ever since they came into the garden.

It was, indeed, a most shady and secluded bench, an ideal seat for any gallant young Baron who had left his Baroness sufficiently far away. He glanced down complacently upon his brawny knees, displayed (he could not but think) to great advantage beneath his kilt and sporran, and then with a tenderer complacency turned his gaze upon his fair companion.

" You say you like me in ze tartan ? " he murmured.

" I adore everything Highland! Oh, Lord Tulli-wuddle, how fortunate you are! "

Nature had gifted Miss Gallosh with a generous share of romantic sentiment. It was she who had egged on her father to rent this Highland castle for the summer, instead of chartering a yacht as he had done for the past few years; and ever since they had come here that sentiment had grown, till she was ready to don the white cockade and plot a new Jacobite uprising. Then, while her heart was in this inspired condition, a noble young chief had stepped in to complete the story. No wonder her dark eyes burned.

" What attachment you must feel for each stone of the Castle!" she continued in a rapt voice. " How your heart must beat to remember that your greatgrandfather—wasn't his name Fergus ? "

" Fergus: yes," said the Baron, blindly but promptly.

" No, no; it was Ian, of course."

" Ach, so! Ian he vas."

" You were thinking of his father," she smiled.

" Yes, his fazzer."

She reflected sagely.

" I am afraid I get my facts mixed up sometimes. Ian—ah, Reginald came before him—not Fergus! "

"Reginald—oh yes, so he did!"
She looked a trifle disappointed.

"If I were you I should know them all by heart," said she.

"I vill learn zem. Oh yes, I most not make soch mistakes."

Indeed he registered a very sincere vow to study his family history that afternoon.

"What was I saying? Oh yes—about your brave great-grandfather. Do you know, Lord Tulliwuddle, I want to ask you a strange favor? You won't think it very odd of me?"

"Odd? Never! Already it is granted."

"I want to hear from your own lips—from the lips of an actual Lord Tulliwuddle—the story of your ancestor Ian's exploit."

With beseeching eyes and a face flushed with a sense of her presumption, she uttered this request in a voice that tore the Baron with conflicting emotions.

"Vich exploit do you mean?" he asked in a kindly voice but with a troubled eye.

"You must know! When he defended the pass, of course."

"Ach, so!"

The Baron looked at her, and though he boasted of no such inventive gifts as his friend Bunker, his ardent heart bade him rather commit himself to perdition than refuse.

"You will tell it tome?"

"I vill!"

Making as much as possible of the raconteur's privileges of clearing his throat, settling himself into good

COUNT BUNKER

position, and gazing dreamily at the tree-tops for inspiration, he began in a slow, measured voice—

"In ze pass he stood. Zen gomed his enemies. He fired his gon and shooted some dead. Zen did zey run avay. Zat vas vat happened."

When he ventured to meet her candid gaze after thus lamely libelling his forefather, he was horrified to observe that she had already recoiled some feet away from him, and seemed still to be in the act of recoiling.

"It would have been kinder to tell me at once that I had asked too much!" she exclaimed in a voice affected by several emotions. "I only wanted to hear you repeat his death-cry as his foes slew him, so that it might always seem more real to me. And you snub me like this!"

The Baron threw himself upon one knee.

"Forgive me! I did jost lose mine head mit your eyes looking so at me! I get confused, you are so lovely! I did not mean to snob!"

In the ardor of his penitence he discovered himself holding her hand; she no longer seemed to be recoiling; and Heaven knows what might have happened next if an ostentatious sound of whistling had not come to their rescue.

"Bot you vill forgive?" he whispered, as they sprang up from their shady seat.

"Ye-es," she answered, just as the serene glance of Count Bunker fell humorously upon them.

"You seem to have been plucking flowers, Tulli-wuddle," he observed.

"Flowers? Oh, no."

The Count glanced pointedly at his soiled knee.

"Indeed!" said he. "Don't I see traces of a flower-bed?"

"I think I should go in," murmured Eva, and she was gone before the Count had time to frame a compensating speech.

His friend Tulliwuddle looked at him with marked displeasure, yet seemed to find some difficulty in adequately expressing it.

"I do not care for vat you said," he remarked stiffly. "Nor for ze look now on your face."

"Baron," said the Count imperturbably, "what did you tell me the Wraith said to you—something about * Beware of the ladies,' wasn't it ? "

"You do not onderstand. Ze ghost" (he found some difficulty in pronouncing the spirit's chosen name) "did soppose naturally zat I vas ze real Lord Tolly-voddle, who is, as you have told me yourself, Bonker, somezing of a fast fish. Ze varning vas to him obviously, so you should not turn it upon me."

Bunker opened his eyes.

"A deuced ingenious argument," he commented. "It wouldn't have occurred to me if you hadn't explained. Then you claim the privilege of wooing whom you wish?"

"Wooing! You forget zat I am married, Bonker."

"Oh no, I remember perfectly."

His tone disturbed the Baron. Taking the Count's arm, he said to him with moving earnestness—

"Have I not told you how constant I am—like ze magnet and ze pole ? "

"I have heard you employ the simile."

"Ach, hot it is true! I am inside my heart so constant as it is possible! But I now represent Tollyvoddle, and for his sake most try to do my best."

Again Count Bunker glanced at his knee.

"And that is your best, then?"

"Listen, Bonker, and try to onderstand—not jost to make jokes. It appears to me zat Miss Gallosh vill make a good vife to Tollyvoddle. She is so fair, so amiable, and so rich. Could he do better? Should I not lay ze foundations of a happy marriage mit her? Soppose ve do get her instead of Miss Mad-dison, eh ? "

His artful eloquence seemed to impress his friend, for he smiled thoughtfully and did not reply at once. More persuasively than ever the Baron continued—

"I do believe mit patience and mit—er—mit kindness, Bonker, I might persuade Miss Gallosh to listen to ze proposal of Tollyvoddle. And vould it not be better far to get him a lady of his own people, and not a stranger from America? Ve vill not like Miss Mad-dison, I feel sure. Vy troble mit her—eh, Bonker ? "

"But don't you think, Baron, that we ought to give Tulliwuddle his choice? He may prefer an American heiress to a Scottish."

"Not if he sees Eva Gallosh!"

Again the Count gently raised his eyebrows in a way that the Baron could not help considering unsuitable to the occasion.

"On the other hand, Baron, Miss Maddison will probably have five or ten times as much money as Miss Gallosh. In arranging a marriage for another man, one must attend to such trifles as a few million dollars more or less."

For the moment the Baron was silenced, but evidently not convinced.

"Supposing I were to call upon the Maddisons as your envoy ? " suggested Bunker, who, to tell the truth, had already begun to tire of a life of luxurious inaction.

" Pairhaps in a few days we might gonsider it."

" We have been here for a week already."

" Ven vould you call? "

" To-morrow, for instance."

The Baron frowned; but argument was difficult.

" You only jost vill go to see? "

" And report to you."

" And suppose she is ogly—or not so nice—or so on zen vill I not see her, eh? "

" But suppose she is tolerable ? "

" Zen vill ve give him a choice, and I vill continue to be polite to Miss Gallosh. Ah, Bonker, she is so nice! He vill not like Miss Maddison so veil! Him-mel, I do admire her ! "

The Baron's eyes shone with reminiscent affection.

" To how many poles is the magnet usually constant ? " inquired the Count with a serious air.

The Baron smiled a little foolishly, and then, with a confidential air, replied—

" Ach, Bonker, marriage is blessed and it is happy, and it is every zing that my heart desires; only I jost sometimes vish it vas not qvite—qvite so uninterrupt-able!"

CHAPTER XVI

IN a dog-cart borrowed from his obliging host, Count Bunker approached the present residence of Mr. Darius P. Maddison. He saw, and—in his client's interest—noted with approval the efforts that were being made to convert an ordinary fishing-lodge into a suitable retreat for a gentleman worth so many million dollars. " Corryvohr," as the house was originally styled, or " Lincoln Lodge," as the patriotic Silver King had re-named it, had already been enlarged for his reception by the addition of four complete suites of apartments, each suitable for a nobleman and his retinue, an organ hall, 10,000 cubic yards of scullery accommodation, and a billiard-room containing three tables. But since he had taken up his residence there he had discovered the lack of several other essentials for a quiet " mountain life " (as he appropriately phrased it), and these defects were rapidly being remedied as our friend drove up. The conservatory was already completed, with the exception of the orchid and palm houses; the aviary was practically ready, and several crates of the rarer humming-birds were expected per goods train that evening; while a staff of electricians could be seen erecting the private telephone by which Mr. Maddison proposed to keep himself in touch with the silver market.

The Count had no sooner pressed the electric bell than a number of men-servants appeared, sufficient to conduct him in safety to a handsome library fitted with polished walnut, and carpeted as softly as the moss on a mountain-side. Having sent in his card, he entertained himself by gazing out of the window and wondering what strange operation was being conducted on a slope above the house, where a grove of pines were apparently being rocked to and fro by a concourse of men with poles and pulleys. But he had not to wait long, for with a promptitude that gave one some inkling of the secret of Mr. Maddison's business success, the millionaire entered.

In a rapid survey the Count perceived a tall man in the neighborhood of sixty: gray-haired, gray-eyed, and gray-faced. The clean-shaved and well-cut profile included the massive foundation of jaw which Bunker had confidently anticipated, and though his words sounded florid in a European ear, they were uttered in a voice that corresponded excellently with this predominant chin.

" I am very pleased to see you, sir, very pleased indeed," he assured the Count not once but several times, shaking him heartily by the hand and eyeing him with a glance accustomed to foresee several days before his fellows the probable fluctuations in the price of anything.

" I have taken the liberty of calling upon you in the capacity of Lord Tulliwuddle's confidential friend," the Count began. " He is at present, as you may perhaps have learned, visiting his ancestral possessions "

" My dear sir, for some days we have been expecting his lordship and yourself to honor us with a visit," Mr. Maddison interposed. " You need not trouble to introduce yourself. The name of Count Bunker is already familiar to us."

He bowed ceremoniously as he spoke, and the Count with no less politeness laid his hand upon his heart and bowed also.

" I looked forward to the meeting with pleasure," he replied. " But it has already exceeded my anticipations."

He would have still further elaborated these assurances, but with his invariable tact he perceived a shrewd look in the millionaire's eye that warned him he had to do with a man accustomed to flowery preliminaries from the astutest manipulators of a deal.

" I am only sorry you should find our little cottage in such disorder," said Mr. Maddison. " The contractor for the conservatory undertook to erect it in a week, and my only satisfaction is that he is now paying me a forfeit of 500 dollars a day. As for the electricians in this country, sir, they are not incompetent men, but they must be taught to hustle if they are to work under American orders; and I don't quite see how they are to find a job anyways else."

He turned to the window with a more satisfied air.

" Here, however, you will perceive a tolerably satisfactory piece of work. I guess those trees will be ready pretty near as soon as the capercailzies are ready for them."

Count Bunker opened his eyes.

" Do I understand that you are erecting a pine wood? "

" You do. That fir forest is my daughter's notion. She thought ordinary plane-trees looked kind of unsuitable for our mountain home. The land of Burns and of the ill-fated Claverhouse, Viscount Dundee, should have more appropriate foliage than that! Well, sir, it took four hundred men just three days to remove the last traces of the last root of the last of those plane-trees."

" And the pines, I suppose, you brought from a neighboring wood?" said the Count, patriotically endeavoring not to look too dumbfoundered.

" No, sir. Lord Tulliwuddle's factor was too slow for me—said he must consult his lordship before removing the timber on the estate. I cabled to Norway: the trees arrived yesterday in Aberdeen, and I guess half of them are as near perpendicular by now as a theodolite can make them. They are being erected, sir, on scientific principles."

Restraining his emotion with a severe effort, Bunker quietly observed—

" Very good idea. I don't know that it would have occurred to me to land them at Aberdeen."

From the corner of his eye he saw that his composure had produced a distinct impression, but he found it hard to retain it through the Silver King's next statement.

" You have taken a long lease of Lincoln Lodge, I presume ? " he inquired.

" One year," said Mr. Maddison. " But I reckon to be comfortable if I'm spending twenty minutes at a railroad junction."

" Ah! " responded the Count, " in that case shifting a forest must be child's-play."

The millionaire smiled affably at this pleasantry and invited his guest to be seated.

" You will try something American, I hope, Count Bunker ? " he asked, touching the bell.

Count Bunker, rightly conceiving this to indicate a cock-tail, replied that he would, and in as nearly seven and a half seconds as he could calculate, a tray appeared with two of these remarkable compounds. Following his host's example, the Count threw his down at a gulp.

" The same," said Mr. Maddison simply. And in an almost equally brief space the same arrived.

" Now," said he, when they were alone again, " I hope you will pardon me, Count, if I am discourteous enough to tell you that my time is uncomfortably cramped. When I first came here I found that I was expected to stand upon the shore of the river for two hours on the chance of catching one salmon. But I have changed all that. As soon as I step outside my door, my ghillie brings me my rod, and if there ain't a salmon at the end for me to land, another ghillie will receive his salary. Since lunch I have caught a fish, despatched fifteen cablegrams, and dictated nine letters. I am only on holiday here, and if I don't get through double that amount in the next two hours I scarcely see my way to do much more fishing to-day. That being so, let us come right to the point. You bring some kind of proposition from Lord Tulliwuddle, I guess?"

During his drive the Count had cogitated over a number of judicious methods of opening the delicate business; but his adaptability was equal to the occasion. In as business-like a tone as his host, he replied—

" You are quite right, Mr. Maddison. Lord Tulliwuddle has deputed me to open negotiations for a certain matrimonial project."

Mr. Maddison's expression showed his appreciation of this candor and delicacy.

" Well," said he, " to be quite frank, Count, I should have thought all the better of his lordship if he had been a little more prompt about the business."

" It is not through want of admiration for Miss Maddison, I assure you "

" No," interrupted Mr. Maddison, " it is because he does not realize the value of time—which is considerably more valuable than admiration, I can assure you. Since I discussed the matter with Lord Tulliwuddle's aunt we have had several more buyers — I should say, suitors—in the market—er— in the field, Count Bunker. But so far, fortunately for his lordship, my Eleanor has not approved of the samples sent, and if he still cares to come forward we shall be pleased to consider his proposition."

The millionaire looked at him out of an impenetrable eye; and the Count in an equally guarded tone replied—

" I greatly approve of putting things on so sound a footing, and with equal frankness I may tell you— in confidence, of course—that Lord Tulliwuddle also is not without alternatives. He would, however, prefer to offer his title and estates to Miss Maddison, provided that there is no personal objection to be found on either side."

Mr. Maddison's eye brightened and his tone warmed.

" Sir," said he, " I guess there won't be much objection to Eleanor Maddison when your friend has seen her. Without exaggeration, I may say that she is the most beautiful girl in America, and that is to say, the most beautiful girl anywhere. The precise amount of her fortune we can discuss, supposing the necessity arrives: but I can assure you it will be sufficient to set three of your mortgaged British aristocrats upon their legs again. No, sir, the objection will not come from that side!"

With a gentle smile and a deprecatory gesture the Count answered, " I am convinced that Miss Maddison is all — indeed, more than all—your eloquence has painted. On the other hand, I trust that you will not be disappointed in my friend Tulliwuddle."

Mr. Maddison crossed his legs and interlocked his fingers like a man about to air his views. This, in fact, was what he proceeded to do.

" My opinion of aristocracies and the pampered individuals who compose them is the opinion of an intelligent and enlightened democrat. I see them from the vantage-ground of a man who has made his own way in the world unhampered by ancestry, who has dwelt in a country fortunately unencumbered by such hindrances to progress, and who has no personal knowledge of their defects. You will admit that I speak with unusual opportunities of forming a judgment?"

" You should have the impartiality of a missionary," said Bunker gravely.

" That is so, sir. Now, in proposing to marry my daughter to a member of this class, I am actuated solely by a desire to take advantage of the opportunities such an alliance would confer. I am still perfectly clear?"

" Perfectly," replied Bunker, with the same profound gravity.

" In consequence," resumed the millionaire, with the impressiveness of a logician drawing a conclusion from two irrefutable premises—" in consequence, Count Bunker, I demand—and my daughter demands—and my son demands, sir, that the nobleman should possess an unusual number of high-class, fire-proof, expert-guaranteed qualities. That is only fair, you must admit?"

" I agree with you entirely."

Mr. Maddison glanced at the clock and sprang to his feet.

" I have not the pleasure of knowing my neighbor, Mr. Gallosh," he said, resuming his brisk business tone; " but I beg you to convey to him and to his wife and daughter my compliments—and my daughter's compliments—and tell them that we hope they will excuse ceremony and bring Lord Tulliwuddle to luncheon to-morrow."

Count Bunker expressed his readiness to carry this message, and the millionaire even more briskly resumed—

" I shall now give myself the pleasure of presenting you to my son and daughter."

With his swiftest strides he escorted his distinguished guest to another room, flung the door open, announced, " My dears, Count Bunker!" and pressed the Count's hand even as he was effecting this introduction.

" Very pleased to have met you, Count. Good day," he ejaculated, and vanished on the instant.

RAISING his eyes after the profound bow which the Count considered appropriate to his character of plenipotentiary, he beheld at last the object of his mission; and whether or not she was the absolutely peerless beauty her father had vaunted, he at once decided that she was lovely enough to grace Hechnahoul, or any other, Castle. Black eyes and a mass of coal-black hair, an ivory pale skin, small well-chiselled features, and that distinctively American plumpness of contour—these marked her face; while as for her figure, it was the envy of her women friends and the distraction of all mankind who saw her.

" Fortunate Baron! " thought Bunker.

Beside her, though sufficiently in the rear to mark the relative position of the sexes in the society they adorned, stood Darius P. Maddison, junior—or " Ri," in the phrase of his relatives and friends—a broad-shouldered, well-featured young man, with keen eyes, a mouth compressed with the stern resolve to die richer than Mr. Rockefeller, and a pair of perfectly ironed trousers.

" I am very delighted to meet you," declared the heiress.

" Very honored to have this pleasure," said the brother.

" While I enjoy both sensations," replied the Count, with his most agreeable smile.

A little preliminary conversation ensued, in the course of which the two parties felt an increasing satisfaction in one another's society; while Bunker had the further pleasure of enjoying a survey of the room in which they sat. Evidently it was Miss Maddison's peculiar sanctum, and it revealed at once her taste and her power of gratifying it. The tapestry that covered two sides of the room could be seen at a glance to be no mere modern imitation, but a priceless relic of the earlier middle ages. The other walls were so thickly hung with pictures that one could scarcely see the pale-green satin beneath; and among these paintings the Count's educated eye recognized the work of Raphael, Botticelli, Turner, and Gainsborough among other masters; while beneath the cornice hung a well-chosen selection from the gems of the modern Anglo-American school. The chairs and sofa were upholstered in a figured satin of a slightly richer hue of green, and on several priceless oriental tables lay displayed in ivory, silver, crystal, and alabaster more articles of vertu than were to be found in the entire house of an average collector.

" Fortunate Tulliwuddle! " thought Bunker.

They had been conversing on general topics for a few minutes, when Miss Maddison turned to her brother and said, with a frankness that both pleased and entertained the Count —

COUNT BUNKER

" Ri, dear, don't you think we had better come right straight to the point? I feel sure Count Bunker is only waiting till he knows us a little better, and I guess it will save him considerable embarrassment if we begin."

" You are the best judge, Eleanor. I guess your notions are never far off being all right."

With a gratified smile Eleanor addressed the Count.

" My brother and I are affinities," she said. " You can speak to him just as openly as you can to me. What is fit for me to hear is fit for him."

Assuring her that he would not hesitate to act upon this guarantee if necessary, the Count nevertheless diplomatically suggested that he would sooner leave it to the lady to open the discussion.

" Well," she said, " I suppose we may presume you have called here as Lord Tulliwuddle's friend? "

" You may, Miss Maddison."

" And no doubt he has something pretty definite to suggest? "

" Matrimony," smiled the Count.

Her brother threw him a stern smile of approval.

" That's right slick there! " he exclaimed.

" Lord Tulliwuddle has made a very happy selection in his ambassador," said Eleanor, with equal cordiality. " People who are afraid to come to facts tire me. No doubt you will think it strange and forward of me to talk in this spirit, Count, but if you'd had to go through the worry of being an American heiress in a

European state you would sympathize. Why, I'm hardly ever left in peace for twenty-four hours—am I, Ri?"

" That is so," quoth Ri.

" What would you guess my age to be, Count Bunker?"

" Twenty-one," suggested Bunker, subtracting two or three years on general principles.

" Well, you're nearer it than most people. Nineteen on my last birthday, Count!"

The Count murmured his surprise and pleasure, and Ri again declared, " That is so."

" And it isn't the American climate that ages one, but the terrible persecutions of the British aristocracy! I can be as romantic as any girl, Count Bunker; why, Ri, you remember poor Abe Sellar and the stolen shoe-lace ? "

"Guess I do!" said Ri.

" That was a romance if ever there was one! But I tell you, Count, sentiment gets rubbed off pretty quick when you come to a bankrupt Marquis writing three ill-spelled sheets to assure me of the disinterested affection inspired by my photograph, or a divorced Duke offering to read

Tennyson to me if I'll hire a punt!"

" I can well believe it," said the Count sympathetically.

" Well, now," the heiress resumed, with a candid smile that made her cynicism become her charmingly, " you see how it is. I want a man one can respect. even if he is a peer. He may have as many titles as dad has dollars, but he must be a man! "

" That is so," said Ri, with additional emphasis.

" I can guarantee Lord Tulliwuddle as a model for a sculptor and an eligible candidate for canonization," declared the Count.

" I guess we want something grittier than that," said Ri.

" And what there is of it sounds almost too good news to be true," added his sister. " I don't want a man like a stained-glass window, Count; because for one thing I couldn't get him."

" If you specify your requirements we shall do our best to satisfy you," replied the Count imper-turbably.

" Well, now," said Eleanor thoughtfully, " I may just as well tell you that if I'm going to take a peer— and I must own peers are rather my fancy at present —it was Mohammedan pashas last year, wasn't it, Ri? " (" That is so," from Ri.)—" If I am going to take a peer, I must have a man that looks a peer. I've been plagued with so many undersized and round-shouldered noblemen that I'm beginning to wonder whether the aristocracy gets proper nourishment. How tall is Lord Tulliwuddle? "

" Six feet and half an inch."

" That's something more like!" said Ri; and his sister smiled her acquiescence.

" And does he weigh up to it ? " she inquired. " Fourteen, twelve, and three-quarters."

"What's that in pounds, Ri? We don't count people in stones in America."

A tense frown, a nervous twitching of the lip, and in an instant the young financier produced the answer—

" Two hundred and nine pounds all but four ounces."

" Well," said Eleanor, " it all depends on how he holds himself. That's a lot to carry for a young man."

" He holds himself like one of his native pine-trees, Miss Maddison!"

She clapped her hands.

" Now I call that just a lovely metaphor, Count Bunker! " she cried. " Oh, if he's going to look like a pine, and walk like the pipers at the Torrydhulish gathering, and really be a chief like Fergus MacIvor or Roderick Dhu, I do believe I'll actually fall in love with him!"

" Say, Count," interposed Ri, " I guess we've heard he's half German."

" It was indeed in Germany that he learned his thorough grasp of politics, statesmanship, business, and finance, and acquired his lofty ambitions and indomitable perseverance."

" He'll do, Eleanor," said the young man. " That's to say, if he is anything like the prospectus."

His sister made no immediate reply. She seemed to be musing — and not unpleasantly.

At that moment a motor car passed the window.

"My!" exclaimed Eleanor, "I'd quite forgot!

That will be to take the Honorable Stanley to the station. We must say good-by to him, I suppose."

She turned to the Count and added in explanation—

" The last to apply was the Honorable Stanley Pilk-ington—Lord Didcott's heir, you know. Oh, if you could see him, you'd realize what I've had to go through!"

Even as she spoke he was given the opportunity, for the door somewhat diffidently opened and an unhappy-looking young man came slowly into the room. He was clearly to be classified among the round-shouldered ineligibles; being otherwise a tall and slender youth, with an amiable expression and a smoothly well-bred voice.

" I've come to say good-by, Miss Maddison," he said, with a mournful air. " I—I've enjoyed my visit very much," he added, as he timidly shook her hand.

" So glad you have, Mr. Pilkington," she replied cordially. " It has been a very great pleasure to entertain you. Our friend Count Bunker— Mr. Pilkington."

The young man bowed with a look in his eye that clearly said—

" The next candidate, I perceive."

Then having said good-by to Ri, the Count heard him murmur to Eleanor—

"Couldn't you—er—couldn't you just manage to see me off? "

" With very great pleasure! " she replied in a hearty

voice that seemed curiously enough rather to damp than cheer his drooping spirits.

No sooner had they left the room together than Darius, junior, turned energetically to his guest, and said in a voice ringing with pride—

" You may not believe me, Count, but I assure you that is the third fellow she has seen to the door inside a fortnight! One Duke, one Viscount—who will expand into something more considerable some day—and this Honorable Pilkington! Your friend, sir, will be a fortunate man if he is able to please my sister."

" She seems, indeed, a charming girl."

" Charming! She is an angel in human form! And I, sir, her brother, will see to it that she is not deceived in the man she chooses—not if I can help it! "

The young man said this with such an air as Bunker supposed his forefathers to have worn when they hurled the tea into Boston harbor.

" I trust that Lord Tulliwuddle, at least, will not fall under your displeasure, sir," he replied with an air of sincere conviction that exactly echoed his thoughts.

" Oh, Ri !" cried Eleanor, running back into the room, " he was so sweet as he said good-by in the hall that I nearly kissed him ! I would have, only it might have made him foolish again. But did you see his shoulders, Count! And oh, to think of marrying a gentle thing like that! Is Lord Tulliwuddle a firm man, Count Bunker ? "

"Adamant—when in the right," the Count assured her.

A renewed air of happy musing in her eyes warned him that he had probably said exactly enough, and with the happiest mean betwixt deference and dignity he bade them farewell.

" Then, Count, we shall see you all to-morrow," said Eleanor as they parted. " Please tell your hosts that I am very greatly looking forward to the pleasure of knowing them. There is a Miss Gallosh, isn't there? "

The Count informed her that there was in fact such a lady.

" That is very good news for me! I need a girl friend very badly, Count; these proposals lose half their fun with only Ri to tell them to. I intend to make a confidante of Miss Gallosh on the spot!"

" H'm," thought the Count, as he drove away, " I wonder whether she will."

AS the plenipotentiary approached the Castle he was somewhat surprised to pass a dog-cart containing not only his fellow-guest, Mr. Cromarty-Gow, but Mr. Gow's luggage also, and although he had hitherto taken no particular interest in that gentleman, yet being gifted with the true adventurer's instinct for promptly investigating any unusual circumstance, he sought his host as soon as he reached the house, with a view to putting a careless question or two. For no one, he felt sure, had been expected to leave for a few days to come.

"Yes," said Mr. Gallosh, "the young spark's off verra suddenly. We didn't expect him to be leaving before Tuesday. But —well, the fact is—umh'm—oh, it's nothing to speak off."

This reticence, however, was easily oajoled away by the insidious Count, and at last Mr. Gallosh frankly confided to him—

" Well, Count, between you and me he seems to have had a kind of fancy for my daughter Eva, and then his lordship coming—well, you'll see for yourself how it was."

" He considered his chances lessened? "

131

" Re told Rentoul they were clean gone."

Count Bunker looked decidedly serious.

" The devil! " he reflected. " The Baron is exceeding his commission. Tulliwuddle is a brisk young fellow, but to commit him to two marriages is neither Christian nor kind. And, without possessing the Baron's remarkable enthusiasm for the sex, I feel sorry for whichever lady is not chosen to cut the cake."

He inquired for his friend, and was somewhat relieved to learn that though he had gone out on the loch with Miss Gallosh, they had been accompanied by her brothers and sisters.

"We still have half an hour before dressing," he said. " I shall stroll down and meet them."

His creditable anxiety returned when, upon the path to the loch shore, he met the two Masters and the two younger Misses Gallosh returning without their sister.

" Been in different boats, have you? " said he, after they had explained this curious circumstance; " well, I hope you all had a good sail."

To himself he uttered a less philosophical comment, and quickened his stride perceptibly. He reached the shore, but far or near was never a sign of boat upon the waters.

" Have they gone down! " he thought.

Just then he became aware of a sound arising from beneath the wooded bank a short distance away. It was evidently intended to be muffled, but the Baron's lungs were powerful, and there was no mistaking his deep voice as he sang—

" ' My lofF she's like a red, red rose

Zat's newly sprong in June I My loff she's like a melody Zat's sveetly blayed in tune !'

Ach, how does he end? "

Before his charmer had time to prompt him, the Count raised his own tolerably musical voice and replied—

"' And fare thee weel, my second string !

And fare thee weel awhile ! I won't come back again, my love, For 'tis ower mony mile !"

For an instant there followed a profound silence, and then the voice of the Baron replied, with somewhat forced mirth—

" Vary goot, Bonker! Ha, ha! Vary goot! "

Meanwhile Bunker, without further delay, was pushing his way through a tangle of shrubbery till in a moment he spied the boat moored beneath the leafy bank, and although it was a capacious craft he observed that its two occupants were both crowded into one end.

" I am sent to escort you back to dinner," he said blandly.

" Tell zem ve shall be back in three minutes," replied the Baron, making a prodigious show of preparation for coming ashore.

" I am sorry to say that my orders were strictly to escort, not to herald you," said the Count apologetically.

Fortifying himself against unpopularity by the consciousness that he was doing his duty, this well-principled, even if spurious, nobleman paced back towards the house with the lady between him and the indignant Baron.

"Well, Tulliwuddle," he discoursed, in as friendly a tone as ever, " I left your cards with our American neighbors."

" So? " muttered the Baron stolidly.

" They received me with open arms, and I have taken the liberty of accepting on behalf of Mr., Mrs., and Miss Gallosh, and of our two selves, a very cordial invitation to lunch with them to-morrow."

" Impossible! " cried the Baron gruffly.

Eva turned a reproachful eye upon him.

"Oh, Lord Tulliwuddle! I should so like to go."

The Baron looked at her blankly.

"You vould!"

" I have heard they are such nice people, and have such a beautiful place! "

" I can confirm both statements," said the Count heartily.

" Besides, papa and mamma would be very disappointed if we didn't go."

" Make it as you please," said the Baron gloomily.

His unsuspicious hosts heard of the invitation with such outspoken pleasure that their honored guest could not well renew his protest. He had to suffer the arrangement to be made; but that night when he and Bunker withdrew to their own room, the Count perceived the makings of an argumentative evening.

" Sometimes you interfere too moch," the Baron began without preamble.

" Do you mind being a little more specific ? " replied the Count with smiling composure.

" Zere vas no hurry to lonch mit Maddison."

" I didn't name the date."

" You might have said next veek."

" By next week Miss Maddison may be snapped up by some one else."

" Zen vould Tollyvoddle be more lucky! I have nearly got for him ze most charming girl, mit as moch money as he vants. Ach, you do interfere! You should gon-sider ze happiness of Tollyvoddle."

"That is the only consideration that affects yourself, Baron?"

" Of course! I cannot marry more zan vonce." (Bunker thought he perceived a symptom of a sigh.) " And I most be faithful to Alicia. I most! Ach, yes, Bonker, do not fear for me! I am so constant as—ach, I most keep faithful! "

As he supplied this remarkable testimony to his own fidelity, the Baron paced the floor with an agitation that clearly showed how firmly his constancy was based.

Nevertheless the Count was smiling oddly at something he espied upon the mantelpiece, and stepping up to it he observed—

" Here is a singular phenomenon—a bunch of white heather that has got itself tied together with ribbon! "

The Baron started, and took the tiny bouquet from his hand, his eyes sparkling with delight.

" It must be a gift from " he began, and then laid it down again, though his gaze continued fixed upon it. " How did it gom in ? " he mused. " Ach! she most have brought it herself. How vary nice! "

He turned suddenly and met his friend's humorous eyes.

" I shall be faithful, Bonker! You can trust me! " he exclaimed; " I shall put it in my letter to Alicia, and send it mit my love! See, Bonker! "

He took a letter from his desk—its envelope still open—hurriedly slipped in the white heather, and licked the gum while his resolution was hot. Then, having exhibited this somewhat singular evidence of his constancy, he sighed again.

" It vas ze only safe vay," he said dolefully. " Vas I not right, Bonker? "

" Quite, my dear Baron," replied the Count sympathetically. " Believe me, I appreciate your self-sacrifice. In fact, it was to relieve the strain upon your too generous heart that I immediately accepted Mr. Mad-dison's invitation for to-morrow."

" How so ? " demanded the Baron with perhaps excusable surprise.

" You will be able to decide at once which is the most suitable bride for Tulliwuddle, and then, if you like, we can leave in a day or two."

" Bot I do not vish to leave so soon! "

" Well then, while you stay, you can at least make sure that you are engaging the affections of the right girl."

Though Bunker spoke with an air of desiring merely to assist his friend, the speech seemed to arouse some furious thinking in the Baron's mind.

For some moments he made no reply, and then at last, in a troubled voice, he said—

" I have already a leetle gommitted Tollyvoddle to Eva. Ach, hot not moch! Still it vas a leetle. Miss Maddison—vat is she like ? "

To the best of his ability the Count sketched the charms of Eleanor Maddison—her enthusiasm for large and manly noblemen, and the probable effects of the Baron's stalwart form set off by the tartan which (in deference, he declared, to the Wraith's injunctions) he now invariably wore. Also, he touched upon her father's colossal fortune, and the genuine Tulliwuddle's necessities.

The Baron listened with growing interest.

" Veil," he said, " I soppose I most make a goot impression for ze sake of Tollyvoddle. For instance, ven we drive up "

"Drive? my dear Baron, we shall march! Leave it to me ; I have a very pretty design shaping in my head."

" Aha ! " smiled the Baron; " my showman again, eh?"

His expression sobered, and he added as a final contribution to the debate—

" But I may tell you, Bonker, I do not eggspect to like Miss Maddison. Ah, my instinct he is vonderful! It vas my instinct vich said. ' Chose Miss Gallosh for Tollyvoddle!'"

^•T IF "T'HILE the Baron was thus loyally doing %/%/ his duty, his Baroness, being ignorant W W of the excellence of his purpose, and knowing only that he had deceived her in one matter, and that the descent to Avernus is easy, .passed a number of very miserable days. That heartbreaking " us both " kept her awake at nights and distraught throughout the day, and when for a little she managed to explain the phrase away, and tried to anchor her trust in Rudolph once more, the vision of the St. Petersburg window overlooking the crops would come to shatter her confidence. She wrote a number of passionate replies, but as the Baron in making his arrangements with his Russian friend had forgotten to provide him with his Scotch address, these letters only reached him after the events of this chronicle had passed into history. Strange to say, her only consolation was that neither her mother nor Sir Justin was able to supply any further evidence of any kind whatsoever. One would naturally suppose that the assistance they had gratuitously given would have made her feel eternally indebted to them; but, on the contrary, she was actually inconsistent enough to resent their head-shakings near-

ly as much as her Rudolph's presumptive infidelity. So that her lot was indeed to be deplored.

At last a second letter came, and with trembling fingers, locked in her room, the forsaken lady tore the curiously bulky envelope apart. Then, at the sight of the enclosure that had given it this shape, her heart lightened once more.

" A sprig of white heather!" she cried. " Ah, he loves me still! "

With eager eyes she next devoured the writing accompanying this token; and as the Baron's head happened to be clearer when he composed this second epistle, and his friend's hints peculiarly judicious, it conveyed so plausible an account of his proceedings, and contained so many expressions of his unaltered esteem, that his character was completely reinstated in her regard.

Having read every affectionate sentence thrice over, and given his exceedingly interesting statements of fact the attention they deserved, she once more took up the little bouquet and examined it more curiously and intently. She even untied the ribbon, when, lo and behold ! there fell a tiny and tightly folded twist of paper upon the floor. Preparing herself for a delicious bit of sentiment, she tenderly unfolded and smoothed it out.

" Verses !" she exclaimed rapturously; but the next instant her pleasure gave place to a look of the extremest mystification.

" What does this mean ? " she gasped.

There was, in fact, some excuse for her perplexity, since the precise text of the enclosure ran thus:

"To LORD TULLIWUDDLE.

« O Chieftain, trample on this heath Which lies thy springing foot beneath ! It can recover from thy tread, And once again uplift its head! But spare, O Chief, the tenderer plant, Because when trampled on, it can't!

"EVA."

Too confounded for coherent speculation, the Baroness continued to stare at this baffling effusion. Who Lord Tulliwuddle and Eva were; why this glimpse into their drama (for such it appeared to be) should be forwarded to her; and where the Baron von Blitzenberg came into the story—these, among a dozen other questions, flickered chaotically through her mind for some minutes. Again and again she studied the cryptogram, till at last a few definite conclusions began to crystallize out of the confusion. That the " tenderer plant " symbolized the lady herself, that she was a person to be regarded with extreme suspicion, and that emphatically the bouquet was never originally intended for the Baroness von Blitzenberg, all became settled convictions. The fact that she knew Tulliwuddle to be an existing peerage afforded her some relief ; yet the longer she pondered on the problem of Rudolph's part in the episode, the more uneasy grew her mind.

Composing her face before the mirror till it resumed its normal round-eyed placidity, she locked the letter and its contents in a safe place, and sought out her mother.

" Did you get any letter, dear, by the last post ? " inquired the Countess as soon as she had entered the room.

"Nothing of importance, mamma."

That so sweet and docile a daughter should stoop to deceit was inconceivable. The Countess merely frowned her disappointment and resumed the novel which she was beguiling the hours between eating and eating again.

"Mamma," said the Baroness presently, "can you tell me whether heather is found in many other European countries?"

The Countess raised her firmly penciled eyebrows.

"In some, I believe. What a remarkable question, Alicia."

"I was thinking about Russia," said Alicia with an innocent air. "Do you suppose heather grows there?"

The Countess remembered the floral symptoms displayed by Ophelia, and grew a trifle nervous.

"My child, what is the matter?"

"Oh, nothing," replied Alicia hastily.

A short silence followed, during which she was conscious of undergoing a curious scrutiny.

66 By the way, mamma," she found courage to ask at length, "do you know anything about Lord Tulli-wuddle?"

Lady Grillyer continued uneasy. These irrelevant questions undoubtedly indicated a mind unhinged.

"I was acquainted with the late Lord Tulliwuddle."

"Oh, he is dead, then?"

"Certainly."

Alicia's face clouded for a moment, and then a ray of hope lit it again.

"Is there a present Lord Tulliwuddle?"

"I believe so. Why do you ask?"

"I heard some one speak of him the other day."

She spoke so naturally that her mother began to feel relieved.

"Sir Justin Wallingford can tell you all about the family, if you are curious," she remarked.

"Sir Justin!"

Alicia recoiled from the thought of him. But presently her curiosity prevailed, and she inquired—

"Does he know them well?"

"He inherited a place in Scotland a number of years a g°> J ou remember. It is somewhere near Lord Tulli-wuddle's place — Hech — Hech — Hech-something-or-other Castle. He was very well acquainted with the last Tulliwuddle."

"Oh," said Alicia indifferently, "I am not really interested. It was mere idle curiosity."

For the greater part of twenty-four hours she kept this mystery locked within her heart, till at last she could contain it no longer. The resolution she came to was both desperate and abruptly taken. At five minutes to three she was resolved to die rather than mention that sprig of heather to a soul; at five minutes past she was on her way to Sir Justin Wallingford's house.

"It may be going behind mamma's back," she said

to herself; "but she went behind mine when she consulted Sir Justin."

It was probably in consequence of her urgent voice and agitated manner that she came to be shown straight into Sir Justin's library, without warning on either side, and thus surprised her counsellor in the act of softly singing a well-known hymn to the accompaniment of a small harmonium. He seemed for a moment to be a trifle embarrassed, and the glance he threw at his footman appeared to indicate an early vacancy in his establishment; but as soon as he had recovered his customary solemnity his explanation reflected nothing but credit upon his character.

" The fact is," said he, " that I am shortly going to rejoin my daughter in Scotland. You are aware of her disposition, Baroness ? "

" I have heard that she is inclined to be devotional."

" She is devotional," answered this excellent man. " I have taken considerable pains to see to it. As your mother and I have often agreed, there is no such safeguard for a young girl as a hobby or mania of this sort."

" A hobby or mania? " exclaimed the Baroness in a pained voice.

Sir Justin looked annoyed. He was evidently surprised to find that the principles inculcated by his old friend and himself appeared to outlive the occasion for which they were intended — to wit, the protection of virgin hearts from undesirable aspirations till calm reason and a husband should render them unnecessary.

" I use the terms employed by the philosophical," he hastened to explain; " but my own opinion is inclined to coincide with yours, my dear Alicia."

This paternal use of her Christian name, coupled with the kindly tone of his justification, encouraged the Baroness to open her business.

" Sir Justin," she began, " can I trust you—may I ask you not to tell my mother that I have visited you ? "

" If you can show me an adequate reason, you may rely upon my discretion," said the ex-diplomatist cautiously, yet with an encouraging smile.

" In some things one would sooner confide in a man than a woman, Sir Justin."

" That is undoubtedly true," he agreed cordially. " You may confide in me, Baroness."

" I have heard from my husband again. I need not show you the letter; it is quite satisfactory—oh, quite, I assure you! Only I found this enclosed with it."

In breathless silence she watched him examine critically first the heather and then the verses.

" Lord Tulliwuddle! " he exclaimed. " Is there anything in the Baron's letter to throw any light upon this?"

" Not one word—not the slightest hint."

Again he studied the paper.

" Oh, what does it mean ? " she cried. " I came to you because you know all about the Tulliwuddles. Where is Lord Tulliwuddle now? "

" I am not acquainted with the present peer," he answered meditatively. " In fact, I know singularly little

about him. I did hear—yes, I heard from my daughter some rumor that he was shortly expected to visit his place in Scotland; but whether he went there or not I cannot say."

" You can find out for me ? "

" I shall lose no time in ascertaining."

The Baroness thanked him effusively, and rose to depart with a mind a little comforted.

" And you won't tell mamma ? "

" I never tell a woman anything that is of any importance."

The Baroness was confirmed in her opinion that Sir Justin was not a very nice man, but she felt an increased confidence in his judgment.

CHAPTER XX

FROM the gargoyled keep which the cultured enthusiasm of Eleanor and the purse of her father had recently erected at Lincoln Lodge, the brother and sister looked over a bend of the river, half a mile of valley road, a wave of forest country, and the greater billows of the bare hillsides towering beyond. But out of all this prospect it was only upon the stretch of road that their eyes were bent.

" Surely one should see their carriage soon! " exclaimed Eleanor.

" Seems to me," said her brother, " that you're sitting something like a cat on the pounce for this Tulliwuddle fellow. Why, Eleanor, I never saw you so excited since the first duke came along. I thought that had passed right off."

" Oh, Ri, I was reading ' Waverley ' again last night, and somehow I felt the top of the keep was the only place to watch for a chief! "

" Why, you don't expect him to be different from other people ? "

" Ri! I tell you I'll cry if he looks like any one I've ever seen before! Don't you remember the Count said he moved like a pine in his native forests ? "

" He won't make much headway like that," said Ri

incisively. " I'd sooner he moved like something more spry than a tree. I guess that Count was talking through his hat."

But his sister was not to be argued out of her exalted mood by such prosaic reasoning. She exclaimed at his sluggish imagination, reiterated her faith in the insinuating count's assurances, and was only withheld from sending her brother down for a spy-glass by the reflection that she could not remember reading of its employment by any maiden in analogous circumstances.

It was at this auspicious moment, when the heart of the expectant heiress was inflamed with romantic fancies and excited with the suspense of waiting, and before it had time to cool through any undue delay, that a little cloud of dust first caught her straining eyes.

" He comes at last! " she cried.

At the same instant the faint strains of the pibroch were gently wafted to her embattled tower.

" He is bringing his piper! Oh, what a duck he is! "

" Seems to me he is bringing a dozen of them," observed Ri.

" And look, Ri ! The sun is glinting upon steel! Claymores, Ri ! oh, how heavenly! There must be fifty men! And they are still coming! I do believe he has brought the whole clan! "

Too petrified with delight to utter another exclamation, she watched in breathless silence the approach of a procession more formidable than had ever escorted a Tulliwuddle since the year of Culloden. As they drew nearer, her ardent gaze easily distinguished a stalwart

figure in plaid and kilt, armed to the teeth with target and claymore, marching with a stately stride fully ten paces before his retinue.

" The chief! " she murmured.

Now indeed she saw there was no cause to mourn, for any one at all resembling the Baron von Blitzenberg as he appeared at that moment she had certainly never met before. Intoxicated with his finery and with the terrific peals of melody behind him, he pranced rather than walked up to the portals of Lincoln Lodge, and there, to the amazement and admiration alike of his clansmen and his expectant host, he burst forth into the following Celtic fragment, translated into English for the occasion by his assiduous friend from a hitherto undiscovered manuscript of Ossian:

" I am ze chieftain, Nursed in ze mountains, Behold me, Mac—ig—ig—ig ish !"

(Yet the Count had written this word very distinctly.)

" Oich for ze claymore ! Hoch for ze philabeg! Sons of ze red deers, Children of eagles, I will supply you Mit Sassenach carcases !"

At this point came a momentary lull, the chieftain's eyes rolling bloodthirstily, but the rhapsody having

apparently become congested within his fiery heart. His audience, however, were not given time to recover their senses, before a striking-looking individual, adorned with tartan trews and a feathered hat, in whom all were pleased to recognize Count Bunker, whispered briefly in his lordship's ear, and like a river in spate he foamed on:

" Donald and Ronald Avake from your slumbers ! Maiden so lovely, Smile mit your bright eyes ! Ze heather is blooming ! Ze vild cat is growling ! Hech Dummeldirroch! Behold Tollyvoddle, Ze Lord of ze Mountains ! "

Hardly had the reverberations of the chieftain's voice died away, when the Count, uttering a series of presumably Gaelic cries, advanced with the most dramatic air, and threw his broadsword upon the ground. The Baron laid his across it, the pipes struck up a less formidable, but if anything more exciting air, and the two noblemen, springing simultaneously from the ground, began what the Count confidently trusted their American hosts would accept as the national sword-dance.

This lasted for some considerable time, and gave the Count an opportunity of testifying his remarkable agility and the Baron of displaying the greater part

of his generously proportioned limbs, while the lung power of both became from that moment proverbial in the glen.

At the conclusion of this ceremony the chieftain, crimson, breathless, and radiant, a sight for gods and ladies, advanced to greet his host.

" Very happy to see you, Lord Tulliwuddle," said Mr. Maddison. " Allow me to offer you my very sincere congratulations on your exceedingly interesting exhibition. Welcome to Lincoln Lodge, your lordship! My daughter—my son."

Eleanor, almost as flushed as the Baron by her headlong rush from the keep at the conclusion of the sword-dance, threw him such a smile as none of her admirers had ever enjoyed before; while he, incapable of speech beyond a gasped " Ach!" bowed so low that the Count had gently to adjust his kilt. Then followed the approach of the Gallosh family, attired in costumes of Harris tweed and tartan selected and arranged under the artistic eye of Count Bunker, and escorted, to their huge delight, by six picked clansmen. Their formal presentation having been completed by a last skirl on the bagpipes, the whole party moved in procession to the banqueting-hall.

" A complete success, I flatter myself," thought Count Bunker, with excusable complacency.

To the banquet itself it is scarcely possible for a mere mortal historian to pay a fitting tribute. Every rarity known to the gourmet that telegraph could summon to the table in time was served in course upon

course. Even the sweetmeats in the little gold dishes cost on an average a dollar a bon-

bon, while the wine was hardly less valuable than liquid radium. Or at least such was the sworn information subsequently supplied by Count Bunker to the reporter of " The Torry-dhulish Herald."

Eleanor was in her highest spirits. She sat between the Baron and Mr. Gallosh, delighted with the honest pleasure and admiration of the merchant, and all the time becoming more satisfied with the demeanor and conversation of the chief. In fact, the only disappointment she felt was connected with the appearance of Miss Gallosh. Much as she had desired a confidante, she had never demanded one so remarkably beautiful, and she could not but feel that a very much plainer friend would have served her purpose quite as well— and indeed better. Once or twice she intercepted a glance passing between this superfluously handsome lady and the principal guest, until at last it occurred to her as a strange and unseemly thing that Lord Tulli-wuddle should be paying so long a visit to his shooting tenants. Eva, on her part, felt a curiously similar sensation. These American gentlemen were as pleasant as report had painted them, but she now discovered an odd antipathy to American women, or at least to their unabashed method of making themselves agreeable to noblemen. It confirmed, indeed, the worst reports she had heard concerning the way in which they raided the British marriage market.

Being placed beside one of these lovely girls and

opposite the other, the Baron, one would think, would be in the highest state of contentment; but though still flushed with his triumphant caperings over the broadswords, and exhibiting a graciousness that charmed his hosts, he struck his observant friend as looking a trifle disturbed at soul. He would furtively glance across the table and then as furtively throw a sidelong look at his neighbor, and each time he appeared to grow more thoughtful. And yet he did not look precisely unhappy either. In fact, there was a gleam in his eye during each of these glances which suggested that both fell upon something he approved of.

The after-luncheon procedure had been carefully arranged between the two adventurers. The Count was to keep by the Baron's side, and, thus supported, negotiations were to be delicately opened. Accordingly, when the party rose, the Count whispered a word in Mr. Maddison's ear. The millionaire answered with a grave, shrewd look, and his daughter, as if perfectly grasping the situation, led the Galloshes out to inspect the new fir forest. And then the two noblemen and the two Dariuses faced one another over their cigars.

CHAPTER XXI

WELL, gentlemen," said Mr. Maddison, " pleasure is pleasure, and business is business. I guess we mean to do a little of both to-day, if you are perfectly disposed. What do you say, Count? "

" I consider that an occasion selected by you, Mr. Maddison, is not to be neglected."

The millionaire bowed his acknowledgment of the compliment, and turned to the Baron, who, it may be remarked, was wearing an expression of thoughtful gravity not frequently to be noted at Hechnahoul.

" You desire to say a few words to me, Lord Tulli-wuddle, I understand. I shall be pleased to hear them."

With this both father and son bent such earnest brows on the Baron and waited for his answer in such intense silence, that he began to regret the absence of his inspiring pipers.

" I vould like ze honor to address mine—mine "

He threw an imploring glance at his friend, who, without hesitation, threw himself into the breach.

" Lord Tulliwuddle feels the natural diffidence of a lover in adequately expressing his sentiments. I understand that he craves your permission to lay a certain case before a certain lady. I am right, Tulliwuddle? '*

" Pairfectly," said the Baron, much relieved; " to lay a certain case before a certain lady. Zat is so, yes, exactly."

Father and son glanced at one another.

" Your delicacy does you honor, very great honor," said Mr. Maddison; " but business is business, Lord Tulliwuddle, and I should like to hear your proposition more precisely stated. In fact, sir, I like to know just where I am."

" That's just about right," assented Ri.

" I vould perhaps vish to marry her."

" Perhaps! " exclaimed the two together.

Again the Count adroitly interposed—

" You mean that you do not intend to thrust your attentions upon an unwilling lady? "

" Yes, yes; zat is vat I mean."

" I see," said Mr. Maddison slowly. " H'm, yes."

" Sounds what you Scotch call ' canny,' " commented Ri shrewdly.

" Well," resumed the millionaire, " I have nothing to say against that; provided—provided, I say, that you stipulate to marry the lady so long as she has no objections to you. No fooling around—that's all we want to see to. Our time, sir, is too valuable."

" That is so," said Ri.

The Baron's color rose, and a look of displeasure came into his eyes, but before he had time to make a retort that might have wrecked his original's hopes, Bunker said quickly—

" Tulliwuddle places himself in your hands, with the
implicit confidence that one gentleman reposes in another."

Gulping down his annoyance, the Baron assented—

« Yes, I vill do zat."

Again father and son looked at one another, and this time exchanged a nod.

" That, sir, will satisfy us," said Mr. Maddison. " Ri, you may turn off the phonograph."

And thereupon the cessation of a loud buzzing sound, which the visitors had hitherto attributed to flies, showed that their host now considered he had received a sufficient guarantee of his lordship's honorable intentions.

" So far, so good," resumed Mr. Maddison. " I may now inform you, Lord Tulliwuddle, that the reports about you which I have been able to gather read kind of mixed, and before consenting to your reception within my daughter's boudoir we should feel obliged if you would satisfy us that the worst of them are not true — or, at least, sir, exaggerated."

This time the Baron could not restrain an exclamation of displeasure.

" Vat, sir ! " he cried, addressing the millionaire. " Do you examine me on my life! "

" No, sir," said Ri, frowning his most determined frown. " It is to me you will be kind enough to give any explanation you have to offer ! Dad may be the spokesman, but I am the inspirer of these interrogations. My sister, sir, the purest girl in America, the most beautiful creature beneath the star-spangled banner of
Columbia, is not going to be the companion of dissolute idleness and gilded dishonor—not, sir, if I know it."

Too confounded by this unusual warning to think of any adequate retort, the Baron could only stare his sensations; while Mr. Maddison, taking up the conversation the instant his son had ceased, proceeded in a deliberate and impressive voice to say—

" Yes, sir, my son—and I associate myself with him —my son and I, sir, would be happy to learn that it is not the case as here stated " (he glanced at a paper in his hand), " namely, Item 1, that you sup rather too frequently with ladies — I beg your pardon, Count Bunker, for introducing the theme—with ladies of the theatrical profession."

" I! " gasped the Baron. " I do only vish I sometimes had ze cha "

" Tulliwuddle! " interrupted the Count. " Don't let your natural indignation carry you away! Mr. Maddison, that statement is not true. I can vouch for it."

" Ach, of course it is not true," said the Baron more calmly, as he began to realize that it was not his own character that was being aspersed.

" I am very glad to hear it," continued Mr. Maddison, who apparently did not share the full austerity of his son's views, since without further question he hurried on to the next point.

" Item 2, sir, states that at least two West End firms are threatening you with proceedings if you do not discharge their accounts within a reasonable time."

" A lie! " declared the Baron emphatically.

" Will you be so kind as to favor us with the name of the individual who is thus libelling his lordship ? " demanded the Count with a serious air.

Mr. Maddison hastily put the paper back in his pocket, and with a glance checked his son's gesture of protest.

" Guess we'd better pass on to the next thing, Ri. I told you it wasn't any darned use just asking. But you boys always think you know better than your Poppas," said he; and then, turning to the Count, " It isn't worth while troubling, Count; I'll see that these reports get contradicted, if I have to buy up a daily paper and issue it at a halfpenny. Yes, sir, you can leave it to me."

The Count glanced at his friend, and they exchanged a grave look.

" Again we place ourselves in your hands," said Bunker.

Though considerably impressed with these repeated evidences of confidence on the part of two such important personages, their host nevertheless maintained something of his inquisitorial air as he proceeded—

" For my own satisfaction, Lord Tulliwuddle, and meaning to convey no aspersion whatsoever upon your character, I would venture to inquire what are your views upon some of the current topics. Take any one you like, sir, so long as it's good and solid, and let me hear what you have to say about it. What you favor us with will not be repeated beyond this room, but merely regarded by my son and myself as proving that

we afre getting no dunder-headed dandy for our Eleanor, but an article of real substantial value—the kind of thing they might make into a Lord-lieutenant or a Viceroy in a bad year."

Tempting in every way as this suggestion sounded, his lordship nevertheless appeared to find a little initial difficulty in choosing a topic.

" Speak out, sir," said Mr. Maddison in an encouraging tone. " Our standard for noblemen isn't anything remarkably high. With a duke I'd be content with just a few dates and something about model cottages, and, though a baron ought to know a little more than that, still we'll count these feudal bagpipers and that ancestral hop-scotch performance as a kind of set-off to your credit. Suppose you just say a few words on the future of the Anglo-Saxon race. What you've learned from the papers will do, so long as you seem to understand it."

Perceiving that his Teutonic friend looked a trifle dismayed at this selection, Count Bunker suggested the Triple Alliance as an alternative.

" That needs more facts, I guess," said the millionaire ; " but it will be all the more creditable if you can manage it."

The Baron cleared his throat to begin, and as he happened (as the Count was well aware) to have the greatest enthusiasm for this policy, and to have recently read the thirteen volumes of Professor Bungstriimpher on the subject, he delivered a peroration so remarkable alike for its fervor, its facts, and its phenomenal length,

that when, upon a gentle hint from the Count, he at last paused, all traces of objection had vanished from the minds of Darius P. Maddison, senior and junior.

" I need no longer detain you, Lord Tulliwuddle," said the millionaire respectfully. " Ri, fetch your sister into her room. Your lordship, I have received an intellectual treat. I am very deeply gratified, sir. Allow me to conduct you to my daughter's boudoir."

Flushed with his exertions and his triumph though the Baron was, he yet remembered so vividly the ordeal preceding the oration that as they went he whispered in his friend's ear—

" Ah, Bonker, stay mit me, I pray you! If she should ask more questions!"

" Mr. Maddison, ze Count will stay mit me."

Though a little surprised at this arrangement, which scarcely accorded with his lordship's virile appearance and dashing air, Mr. Maddison was by this time too favorably disposed to question the wisdom of any suggestion he might make, and accordingly the two friends found themselves closeted together in Miss Maddison's sanctum awaiting the appearance of the heiress.

" Shall I remain through the entire interview ?" asked the Count.

" Oh yes, mine Bonker, you most! Or——veil, soppose it gets unnecessary zen vill I cry ' By ze Gad!' and you vill know to go."

"'By the Gad'? I see."

" Or—veil, not ze first time, but if I say it tree times, zen vill you make an excuse."

" Three times ? I understand, Baron."

IN the eye of the heiress, as in her father's, might be noted a shade of surprise at finding two gentlemen instead of one. But though the Count instantly perceived his superfluity, and though it had been his greatest ambition throughout his life to add no shade to the dullness with which he frequently complained that life was overburdened, yet his sense of obligation to his friend was so strong that he preferred to bore rather than desert. As the only compensation he could offer, he assumed the most retiring look of which his mobile features were capable, and pretended to examine one of the tables of curios.

" Lord Tulliwuddle, I congratulate you on the very happy impression you have made! " began Eleanor with the most delightful frankness.

But his lordship had learned to fear the Americans, even bearing compliments.

"So?" he answered stolidly.

"Indeed you have! Hi is just wild about your cleverness."

" Zat is kind of him."

" He declares you are quite an authority on European politics. Now you will be able to tell

" Ach, no ! I shall not to-day, please! " interrupted the Baron hurriedly.

The heiress seemed disconcerted.

" Oh, not if you'd rather not, Lord Tulliwuddle."

" Not to-day."

"Well!"

She turned with a shrug and cast her eyes upon the wall.

" How do you like this picture ? It's my latest toy. I call it just sweet!"

He cautiously examined the painting.

" It is vary pretty."

"Do you know Romney's work?"

The Baron shrank back.

" Not again to-day, please! "

Miss Maddison opened her handsome eyes to their widest.

" My word!" she cried. " If these are Highland manners, Lord Tulliwuddle! "

In extreme confusion the Baron stammered—

" I beg your pardon! Forgif me—but—ach, not zose questions, please! "

Relenting a little, she inquired—

" What may I ask you, then ? Do tell me! You see I want just to know all about you."

With an affrighted gesture the Baron turned to his friend.

" Bonker," said he, " she does vant to know yet more about me! Vill you please to tell her."

The Count looked up from the curios with an expression so bland that the air began to clear even before he spoke.

" Miss Maddison, I must explain that my friend's proud Highland spirit has been a little disturbed by some inquiries, made in all good faith by your father. No offence, I am certain, was intended; erroneous information—a little hastiness in jumping to conclusions —a sensitive nature wounded by the least insinuation—such were the unfortunate causes of Tulliwud-dle's excusable reticence. Believe me, if you knew all, your opinion of him would alter very, very considerably !"

The perfectly accurate peroration to this statement produced an immediate effect.

" What a shame!" cried Eleanor, her eyes sparkling brightly. " Lord Tulliwuddle, I am so sorry! "

The Baron looked into these eyes, and his own mien altered perceptibly. For an instant he gazed, and then in a low voice remarked—

"By ze Gad!"

" Once! " counted the conscientious Bunker.

" Lord Tulliwuddle," she continued, " I declare I feel so ashamed of those stupid men, I could just wring their necks! Now, just to make us quits, you ask me anything in the world you like!"

Over his shoulder the Baron threw a stealthy glance at his friend, but this time he did not invoke his assistance. Instead, he again murmured very distinctly—

"By ze Gad!"

" Twice! " counted Bunker.

" Miss Maddison," said the Baron to the flushed and eager girl, " am I to onderstand zat you now are satisfied zat I am not too vicked, too suspeecious, too un-vorthy of your charming society? I do not say I am yet vorthy—bot jost not too bad! "

Had the Baroness at that moment heard merely the intonation of his voice, she would undoubtedly have preferred a Chinese prison.

" Indeed, Lord Tulliwuddle, you may."

" By ze Gad!" announced the Baron, in a voice braced with resolution.

" May I take the liberty of inspecting the aviary ? " said the Count.

" With the very greatest pleasure," replied the heiress kindly.

His last distinct impression as he withdrew was of the Baron giving his mustache a more formidable twirl.

" A very pretty little scene," he reflected, as he strolled out in search of others. " Though, hang me, I'm not sure if it ended in the right man leaving the stage!"

This " second-fiddle feeling," as he styled it humorously to himself, was further increased by the demeanor of Miss Gallosh, to whom he now endeavored to make himself agreeable. Though sharing the universal respect felt for the character and talents of the Count, she was evidently too perturbed at seeing him appear alone to appreciate his society as it deserved. Ever since luncheon poor Eva's heart had been sinking.

The beauty, the assurance, the cleverness, and the charm of the fabulously wealthy American heiress had filled her with vague misgivings even while the gentlemen were safely absent; but when Miss Maddison was summoned away, and her father and brother took her place, her uneasiness vastly increased. Now here was the last buffer removed between the chieftain and her audacious rival (so she already counted her). What drama could these mysterious movements have been leading to?

In vain did Count Bunker exercise his unique powers of conversation. In vain did he discourse on the beauties of nature as displayed in the wooded valley and the towering hills, and the beauties of art as exhibited in the aviary and the new fir forest. Eva's thoughts were too much engrossed with the beauties of woman, and their dreadful consequences if improperly used.

" Is—is Miss Maddison still in the house ? " she inquired, with an effort to put the question carelessly.

" I believe so," said the Count in his kindest voice.

" And—and—that isn't Lord Tulliwuddle with my father, is it?"

" I believe not," said the Count, still more sympathetically.

She could no longer withhold a sigh, and the Count tactfully turned the conversation to the symbolical eagle arrived that morning from Mr. Maddison's native State.

They had passed from the aviary to the flower-garden, when at last they saw the Baron and Eleanor appear. She joined the rest of the party, while he, walking thoughtfully in search of his friend, advanced in their direction. He raised his eyes, and then, to complete Eva's concern, he started in evident embarrassment at discovering her there also. To do him justice, he quickly recovered his usual politeness. Yet she noticed that he detained the Count beside him and showed a curious tendency to discourse solely on the fine quality of the gravel and the advantages of having a brick facing to a garden wall.

" My lord," said Mr. Gallosh, approaching them, " would you be thinking of going soon ? I've noticed Mr. Maddison's been taking out his watch verra frequently."

" Certainly, certainly! " cried my lord. " Oh, ve have finished all ve have come for."

Eva started, and even Mr. Gallosh looked a trifle perturbed.

" Yes," added the Count quickly, " we have a very good idea of the heating system employed. I quite agree with you : we can leave the rest to your engineer."

But even his readiness failed to efface the effects of his friend's unfortunate admission.

Farewells were said, the procession reformed, the pipers struck up, and amidst the heartiest expressions of pleasure from all, the chieftain and his friends marched off to the spot where (out of sight of Lincoln Lodge) the forethought of their manager had arranged that the carriages should be waiting.

" Well," said Bunker, when they found themselves in their room again, " what do you think of Miss Maddison?"

The Baron lit a cigar, gazed thoughtfully and with evident satisfaction at the daily deepening shade of tan upon his knees, and then answered slowly—

" Veil, Bonker, she is not so bad."

" Ah," commented Bunker.

" Bot, Bonker, it is not vat I do think of her. Ach, no! It is not for mein own pleasure. Ach, nein! How shall I do my duty to Tollyvoddle? Zat is vat I ask myself."

" And what answer do you generally return ? "

" Ze answer I make is," said the Baron gravely and with the deliberation the point deserved— " Ze answer is zat I shall vait and gonsider vich lady is ze best for him."

" The means you employ will no doubt include a further short personal interview with each of them? "

" Vun short ! Ach, Bonker, I most investigate mit carefulness. No, no; I most see zem more zan zat."

" How long do you expect the process will take you?"

For the first time the Baron noticed with surprise a shade of impatience in his friend's voice.

" Are you in a horry, Bonker ? "

" My dear Baron, I grudge no man his sport—particularly if he is careful to label it his duty. But, to tell the truth, I have never played gamekeeper for so long before, and I begin to find that picking up your victims and carrying them after you in a bag is less exhilarating to-day than it was a week ago. I wouldn't curtail your pleasure for the world, my dear fellow! But I do ask you to remember the poor keeper."

" My dear friend," said the Baron cordially, " I shall remember! It shall take bot two or tree days to do my duty. I shall not be long."

te A day or two of sober duty, Then, Hoch ! for London, home, and beauty !"

trolled the Count pleasantly.

The Baron did not echo the "Hoch"; but after retaining his thoughtful expression for a few moments, a smile stole over his face, and he remarked in an absent voice—

" Vun does not alvays need to go home to find beauty."

" Yes," said the Count, " I have always held it to be one of the advantages of travel that one learns to tolerate the inhabitants of other lands."

ACH, you are onfair," exclaimed the Baron. " Really ? " said Eva, with a sarcastic intonation he had not believed possible in so sweet a voice.

It was the day following the luncheon at Lincoln Lodge, and they were once more seated in the shady arbor: this time the Count had guaranteed not only to leave them uninterrupted by his own presence, but to protect the garden from all other intruders. Everything, in fact, had presaged the pleasantest of tete-a-tetes. But, alas! the Baron was learning that if Amaryllis pouts, the shadiest corner may prove too warm. Why, he was asking himself, should she exhibit this incomprehensible annoyance? What had he done? How to awake her smiles again?

" I do not forget my old friends so quickly," he protested. " No, I do assure you! I do not onderstand vy you should say so."

" Oh, we don't profess to be old friends, Lord Tul-liwuddle! After all, there is no reason why you shouldn't turn your back on us as soon as you see a newer—and more amusing—

acquaintance."

" But I have not turned my back! "

" We saw nothing else all yesterday."

"Ah, Mees Gallosh, zat is not true! Often did I look at you! "

"Did you? I had forgotten. One doesn't treasure every glance, you know."

The Baron tugged at his mustache and frowned.

" She vill not do for Tollyvoddle," he said to himself.

But the next instant a glance from Eva's brilliant eyes—a glance so reproachful, so appealing, and so stimulating, that there was no resisting it—diverted his reflections into quite another channel.

" Vat can I do to prove zat I am so friendly as ever? " he exclaimed.

" So friendly ? " she repeated, with an innocently meditative air.

" So vary parteecularly friendly! "

Her air relented a little—just enough, in fact, to make him ardently desire to see it relent still further.

" You promise things to me, and then do them for other people's benefit."

The Baron eagerly demanded a fuller statement of this abominable charge.

" Well," she said, " you told me twenty times you would show me something really Highland—that you'd kill a deer by torchlight, or hold a gathering of the clans upon the castle lawn. All sorts of things you offered to do for me, and the only thing you have done has been for the sake of your new friends! You gave them a procession and a dance."

" But you did see it too!" he interrupted eagerly.

" As part of your procession," she retorted scornfully. " We felt much obliged to you—especially as you were so attentive to us afterwards! "

" I did not mean to leave you," exclaimed the Baron weakly. " It was jost zat Miss Maddison "

" I am not interested in Miss Maddison. No doubt she is very charming; but, really, she doesn't interest me at all. You were unavoidably prevented from talking to us—that is quite sufficient for me. I excuse you, Lord Tulliwuddle. Only, please, don't make me any more promises."

"Eva! Ach, I most say 'Eva' jost vunce more! I am going to leave my castle, to leave you, and say good-by."

She started and looked quickly at him.

" Bot before I go I shall keep my promise! Ve shall have ze pipers, and ze kilts, and ze dancing, and toss ze caber, and fling ze hammer, and it shall be on ze castle lawn, and all for your sake! Vill you not forgive me and be friends? "

"Will it really be all for my sake? "

She spoke incredulously, yet looked as if she were willing to be convinced.

"I swear it vill!"

The latter part of this interview was so much more agreeable than the beginning that when the distant rumble of the luncheon gong brought it to an end at last they sighed, and for fully half a minute lingered still in silence. If one may dare to express in crude language a maiden's unspoken, formless thought, Eva's might be read —" There is yet a moment left for him to say the three short words that seem to hang upon his tongue! " While on his part he was reflecting that he had another duologue arranged for that very afternoon, and that, for the simultaneous suitor of two ladies, an open mind was almost indispensable.

" Then you are going for a drive with the Count Bunker this afternoon ? " she asked, as they strolled slowly towards the house.

" For a leetle tour in my estate," he answered easily.

"On business, I suppose?"

"Yes, vorse luck!"

He knew not whether to feel more relieved or embarrassed to find that he evidently rose in her estimation as a conscientious landlord.

" You are having a capital day's sport, Baron," said the Count gaily, as they drew near Lincoln Lodge.

During their drive the Baron had remained unusually silent. He now roused himself and said in a guarded whisper—

" Bonker, vill you please to give ze coachman some money not to say jost vere he did drive us."

" I have done so," smiled the Count.

His friend gratefully grasped his hand and curled his mustache with an emboldened air.

A similar display of address on the part of Count Bunker resulted in the Baron's finding himself some ten minutes later alone with Miss Maddison in her sane-tuary. But, to his great surprise, he was greeted with none of the encouraging cordiality that had so charmed him yesterday. The lady was brief in her responses, critical in her tone, and evidently disposed to quarrel with her admirer on some ground at present entirely mysterious. Indeed, so discouraging was she that at length he exclaimed—

" Tell me, Miss Maddison— I should not have gom to-day ? You did not vish to see me. Eh ? "

" I certainly was perfectly comfortable without you, Lord Tulliwuddle," said the heiress tartly.

"Shalllgoavay?"

" You have come here entirely for your own pleasure; and the moment you begin to feel tired there is nothing to hinder you going home again."

" You vere more kind to me yesterday," said the Baron sadly.

" I did not learn till after you had gone how much I was to blame for keeping you so long away from your friends. Please do not think I shall repeat the offence."

There was an accent on the word " friends " that enlightened the bewildered nobleman, even though quickness in taking a hint was not his most conspicuous attribute. That the voice of gossip had reached the fair American was only too evident; but though considerably annoyed, he could not help feeling at the same time flattered to see the concern he was able to inspire.

" My friends!" said he with amorous artfulness.

" Do you mean Count Bunker ? He is ze only friend I have here mit me."

" The only friend? Indeed! "

" Zat is since I see you vill not treat me as soch."

Upon these lines a pretty little passage-of-arms ensued, the Baron employing with considerable effect the various blandishments of which he was admitted a past master; the heiress modifying her resentment by degrees under their insidious influence. Still she would not entirely quit her troublesome position, till at last a happy inspiration came to reinforce his assaults. Why, he reflected, should an entertainment that would require a considerable outlay of money and trouble serve to win the affections of only one girl? With the same expenditure of ammunition it might be possible to double the bag.

" Miss Maddison," he said with a regretful air, " I did come here to-day in ze hope But ach! "

So happily had he succeeded in whetting her curiosity that she begged—nay, insisted—that he should finish his sentence.

" If you had been kind I did hope zat you vould allow me to give in your honor an entertainment at my castle."

" An entertainment! " she cried, with a marked increase of interest.

" Jost a leetle exposition of ze Highland sport, mit bagpipes and caber and so forth; unvorthy of your notice perhaps, bot ze best I can do."

Eleanor clapped her hands enthusiastically.

"I should just love it!"

The triumphant diplomatist smiled complacently.

" Bonker vill arrange it all nicely," he said to himself.

And there rose in his fancy such a pleasing and gorgeous picture of himself in the panoply of the North, hurling a hammer skywards amidst the plaudits of his clan and the ravished murmurs of the ladies, that he could not but congratulate himself upon this last master-stroke of policy. For if instead of ladies there were only one lady, exactly half the pleasure would be lacking. So generous were this nobleman's instincts!

During their drive to Lincoln Lodge the Baron had hesitated to broach his new project to his friend for the very reason that, after the glow of his first enthusiastic proposal to Eva was over, it seemed to him a vast undertaking for a limited object; but driving home he lost no time in confiding his scheme to the Count.

" The deuce! " cried Bunker. " That will mean three more days here at least! "

" Vat is tree days, mine Bonker ? "

" My dear Baron, I am the last man in the world to drop an unpleasant hint; yet I can't help thinking we have been so unconscionably lucky up till now that it would be wise to retire before an accident befalls us."

"Vat kind of accident?"

" The kind that may happen to the best regulated adventurer."

The Baron pondered. When Bunker suggested caution it indeed seemed time to beat a retreat; yet— those two charming ladies, and that alluring tartan tableau!

"Ach, let ze devil take ze man zat is afraid!" he exclaimed at last. " Bonker, it vill be soch fun! "

" Watching you complete two conquests ? "

" Be not impatient, good Bonker! "

" My dear fellow, if you could find me one girl— even one would content me—who would condescend to turn her eyes from the dazzling spectacle of Baron Tulliwuddle, and cast them for so much as half an hour a day upon his obscure companion, I might see some fun in it too."

The Baron, with an air of patronizing kindness that made his fellow-adventurer's lot none the easier to bear, answered reassuringly—

" Bot I shall leave all ze preparations to be made by you; you vill not have time zen to feel lonely."

" Thank you, Baron; you have the knack of conferring the most princely favors."

" Ach, I am used to do so," said the Baron simply, and then burst out eagerly, " Some feat you must design for me at ze sports so zat I can show zem my strength, eh?"

" With the caber, for instance? "

The Baron had seen the caber tossed, and he shook his head.

" He is too big."

" I might fit a strong spring in one end."

But the Baron still seemed disinclined. His friend reflected, and then suddenly exclaimed—

" The village doctor keeps some chemical apparatus, I believe! You'll throw the hammer, Baron. I can manage it."

The Baron appeared mystified by the juxtaposition of ideas, but serenely expressed himself as ready to entrust this and all other arrangements for the Hech-nahoul Gathering to the ingenious Count, as some small compensation for so conspicuously outshining him.

CHAPTER XXIV

THE day of the Gathering broke gray and still, and the Baron, who was no weather prophet, declared gloomily—

" It vill rain. Donnerwetter! "

A couple of hours later the sun was out, and the distant hills shimmering in the heat haze.

" Himmel! Ve are alvays lucky, Bonker! " he cried, and with gleeful energy brandished his dumb-bells in final preparation for his muscular exploits.

" We certainly have escaped hanging so far," said the Count, as he drew on the trews which became his well-turned leg so happily.

His arrangements were admirable and complete, and by twelve o'clock the castle lawn looked as barbarically gay as the colored supplement to an illustrated paper. Pipes were skirling, skirts fluttering, flags flapping; and as invitations had been issued to various magnates in the district, whether acquainted with the present peer or not, there were to be seen quite a number of dignified personages in divers shades of tartan, and parasols of all the hues in the rainbow. The Baron was in his element. He judged the bagpipe competition himself, and held one end of the tape that meas-

ured the jumps, besides delighting the whole assembled company by his affability and good spirits.

" Your performance comes next, I see," said Eleanor Maddison, throwing him her brightest smile. " I can't tell you how I am looking forward to seeing you do it! "

The Baron started and looked at the programme in her hand. He had been too excited to study it carefully before, and now for the first time he saw the announcement (in large type)—

" 7. Lord Tulliwuddle throws the 85-lb. hammer."

The sixth event was nearly through, and there— there evidently was the hammer in question being carried into the ring by no fewer than three stalwart Highlanders! The Baron had learned enough of the pastimes of his adopted country to be aware that this gigantic weapon was something like four times as heavy as any hammer hitherto thrown by the hardiest Caledonian.

" Teufel! Bonker vill make a fool of me," he muttered, and hastily bursting from the circle of spectators, hurried towards the Count, who appeared to be busied in keeping the curious away from the Chieftain's hammer.

" Bonker, vat means zis ? " he demanded.

" Your hammer," smiled the Count.

" A hammer zat takes tree men "

"Hush!" whispered the Count. "They are only holding it down! "

The Baron laid his hand upon the round enormous head, and started.

" It is not iron! " he gasped. " It is of rubber."

" Filled with hydrogen," breathed the Count in his ear. " Just swing it once and let go—and, I say, mind it doesn't carry you away with it."

The chief bared his arms and seized the handle; his three clansmen let go ; and then, with what seemed to the breathless spectators to be a merely trifling effort of strength, he dismissed the projectile upon the most astounding journey ever seen even in that land of brawny hammer-hurlers. Up, up, up it soared, over the trees; high above the topmost turret of the castle, and still on and on and ever upwards till it became a mere speck in the zenith, and at last faded utterly from sight.

Then, and not till then, did the pent-up applause break out into such a roar of cheering as Hechnahoul had never heard before in all its long history.

" Eighty-five pounds of pig-iron gone straight to heaven ! " gasped the Silver King. " Guess that beats all records!"

" America must wake up! " frowned Ri.

Meanwhile the Baron, after bowing in turn towards all points of the compass, turned confidentially to his friend.

" Vill not ze men that carried it ? "

" I've told 'em you'd give 'em a couple of sovereigns apiece."

The Baron came from an economical nation.

"Two to each!"

" My dear fellow, wasn't it worth it ? "

The Baron grasped his hand.

" Ja, mine Bonker, it vas! I vill pay zem."

Radiant and smiling, he returned to receive the congratulations of his guests, dreaming that his triumph was complete, and that nothing more arduous remained than pleasant dalliance alternately with his Eleanor and his Eva. But he speedily discovered that hurling an inflated hammer heavenwards was child's play as compared with the simultaneous negotiation of a double wooing. The first person to address him was the millionaire, and he could not but feel a shiver of apprehension to note that he was evidently in the midst of a conversation with Mr. Gallosh.

" I must congratulate you, Lord Tulliwuddle," said Mr. Maddison, " and I must further congratulate my daughter upon the almost miraculous feat you have performed for her benefit. You know, I dare say " —here he turned to Mr. Gallosh—" that this very delightful entertainment was given primarily in my Eleanor's honor?"

" Whut! " exclaimed the merchant. " That's—eh— that's scarcely the fac's as we've learned them. But his lordship will be able to tell you best himself."

His lordship smiled affably upon both, murmured something incoherent, and passed on hastily towards the scarlet parasol of Eleanor. But he had no sooner reached it than he paused and would have turned had she not seen him, for under a blue parasol beside her he espied, too late, the fair face of Eva, and too clearly perceived that the happy maidens had been comparing notes, with the result that neither looked very happy now.

" I hope you do enjoy ze sports," he began, endeavoring to distribute this wish as equally as possible.

" Miss Gallosh has been remarkably fortunate in her weather," said Eleanor, and therewith gave him an uninterrupted view of her sunshade.

" Miss Maddison has seen you to great advantage, Lord Tulliwuddle," said Eva, affording him the next instant a similar prospect of silk.

The unfortunate chief recoiled from this ungrateful reception of his kindness. Only one refuge, one mediator, he instinctively looked for; but where could the Count have gone?

" Himmel ! Has he deserted me ? " he muttered, frantically elbowing his way in search of him.

But this once it happened that the Count was engaged upon business of his own. Strolling outside the ring of spectators, with a view to enjoying a cigar and a little relaxation from the anxieties of stage-management, his attention had been arrested in a singular and flattering way. At that place where he happened to be passing stood an open carriage containing a girl and an older lady, evidently guests from the neighborhood personally unknown to his lordship, and just as he went by he heard pronounced in a thrilling whisper—" That must be Count Bunker! "

The Count was too well-bred to turn at once, but it is hardly necessary to say that a few moments later he casually repassed the carriage; nor will it astonish any who have been kind enough to follow his previous career with some degree of attention to learn that when opposite the ladies he paused, looked from them to the enclosure and back again, and presently raising his feathered bonnet, said in the most ingratiating tones—

" Pardon me, but I am requested by Lord Tulli-wuddle to show any attention I can to the comfort of his guests. Can you see well from where you are? "

The younger lady with an eager air assured him that they saw perfectly, and even in the course of the three or four sentences she spoke he was able to come to several conclusions regarding her: that her companion was in a subsidiary and doubtless salaried position; that she herself was decidedly attractive to look upon; that her voice had spoken the whispered words ; and that her present animated air might safely be attributed rather to the fact that she addressed Count Bunker than to the subject-matter of her reply.

No one possessed in a higher degree than the Count the nice art of erecting a whole conversation upon the foundation of the lightest phrase. He contrived a reply to the lady's answer, was able to put the most natural question next, to follow that with a happy stroke of wit, and within three minutes to make it seem the most obvious thing in the world that he should be saying—

" I am sure that Lord Tulliwuddle will never forgive me if I fail to learn the names of any visitors who have honored him to-day."

" Mine," said the girl, her color rising slightly, but her glance as kind as ever, " is Julia Wallingf ord. This is my friend Miss Minchell."

The Count bowed.

" And may I introduce myself as a friend of Tulli-wuddle's, answering to the name of Count Bunker."

Again Miss Wallingford's color rose. In a low and ardent voice she began—

" I am so glad to meet you! Your name is already "

But at that instant, when the Count was bending forward to catch the words and the lady bending down to utter them, a hand grasped him by the sleeve, and the Baron's voice exclaimed—

" Come, Bonker, quickly here to help me! "

He would fain have presented his lordship to the ladies, but the Baron was too hurried to pause, and with a parting bow he was reluctantly borne off to assist his friend out of his latest dilemma.

"Pooh, my dear Baron!" he cried, when the situation was explained to him; "you couldn't have done more damage to their hearts if you had hurled your hammer at them! A touch of jealousy was all that was needed to complete your conquests. But for me you have spoiled the most promising affair imaginable. There goes their carriage trotting down the drive! And I shall probably never know whether my name was already in her heart or in her prayers. Those are the two chief receptacles for gentlemen's names, I believe —aren't they, Baron?"

On his advice the rival families were left to the soothing influences of a good dinner and a night's sleep, and he found himself free to ponder over his interrupted adventure.

"Undoubtedly one feels all the better for a little appreciation," he reflected complacently. "I wonder if it was my trews that bowled her over?"

CHAPTER XXV

THE Count next morning consumed a solitary breakfast, his noble friend having risen some hours previously and gone for an early walk upon the hill. But he was far from feeling any trace of boredom, since an open letter beside his plate appeared to provide him with an ample fund of pleasant and entertaining reflections.

"I have not withered yet," he said to himself. "Here is proof positive that some blossom, some aroma remains!"

The precise terms of this encouraging epistle were these:

'"THE LASH, near NETHERBRIO. "Tuesday night.

"DEAR COUNT BUNKER,—Forgive what must seem to you incredible boldness (!), and do not think worse of me than I deserve. It seems such a pity that you should be so near and yet that I should lose this chance of gratifying my great desire. If you knew how I prized the name of Bunker you would understand; but no doubt I am only one among many, and you do understand better than I can explain.

"My father is away from home, and the world dictates prudence; but I know your views on conventionality are those I too have learned to share, so will you come and see me before you leave Scotland?

"With kindest regards and in great haste because I want you to get this to-morrow morning. Believe me, yours very sincerely,

"JULIA WALLINGFORD."

"P.S.—If it would upset your arrangements to come only for the day, Miss Minchell agrees with me that we could easily put you up.—J. W."

"By Jingo!" mused the Count, "that's what I call a sporting offer. Her father away from home, and Count Bunker understanding better than she can explain! Gad, it's my duty to go!"

But besides the engaging cordiality of Miss Wallingford's invitation, there was something about the letter that puzzled almost as much as it cheered him.

"She prizes the name of Bunker, does she? Never struck me it was very ornamental; and in any case the compliment seems a trifle stretched. But, hang it! this is looking a gift-horse in the mouth. Such ardor deserves to be embraced, not dissected."

He swiftly debated how best to gratify the lady. Last night it had been his own counsel, and likewise the Baron's desire, to leave by the night mail that very evening, with their laurels still unfaded and blessings heaped upon their heads. Why not make his next stage The Lash?

"Hang it, the Baron has had such a good innings that he can scarcely grudge me a short knock," he said to himself. "He can wait for me at Perth or somewhere."

And, ringing the bell, he wrote and promptly despatched this brief telegram:

" Delighted. Shall spend to-night in passing. Bunker."

Hardly was this point settled when the footman re-entered to inform him that Mr. Maddison's motor car was at the door waiting to convey him without delay to Lincoln Lodge. Accompanying this announcement came the Silver King's card bearing the words, " Please come and see me at once."

The Count stroked his chin, and lit a cigarette.

" There is something fresh in the wind," thought he.

In the course of his forty-miles-an-hour rush through the odors of pine woods, he had time to come to a pretty correct conclusion regarding the business before him, and was thus enabled to adopt the mien most suitable to the contingency when he found himself ushered into the presence of the millionaire and his son. The set look upon their faces, the ceremonious manner of their greeting, and the low buzzing of the phonograph, audible above the tinkle of a musical box ingeniously intended to drown it, confirmed his guess even before a word had passed.

" Be seated, Count," said the Silver King ; and the Count sat.

" Now, sir," he continued, " I have sent for you,

owing, sir, to the high opinion I have formed of your intelligence and business capabilities."

The Count bowed profoundly.

" Yes, sir, I believe, and my son believes, you to be a white man, even though you are a Count."

" That is so," said Ri.

" Now, sir, you must be aware—in fact, you are aware — of the matrimonial project once entertained between my daughter and Lord Tulliwuddle."

" Once! " exclaimed the Count in protest.

" Once! " echoed Ri in his deepest voice.

" Hish, Ri! Let your poppa do the talking this time," said the millionaire sternly, though with an indulgent eye.

" But—er— once? " repeated the Count, as if bewildered by the past tense implied; though to himself he murmured—" I knew it! "

" When I gave my sanction to Lord Tulliwuddle's proposition, I did so under the impression that I was doing a deal with a man, sir, of integrity and honor. But what do I find?"

" Yes, what? " thundered Ri.

" I find, sir, that his darned my-lordship— and be damned to his titles "

" Mr. Maddison! " expostulated the Count gently.

" I find, Count, I find that Lord Tulliwuddle, under pretext of paying my Eleanor a compliment, has provided an entertainment—a musical and athletic entertainment — for another woman ! "

The Count sprang to his feet.

" Impossible! " he cried.

"It is true!"

"Name her!"

" She answers, sir, to the plebeian cognomen of Gal-losh."

" A nobody! " sneered Ri.

" In trade! " added his father scornfully.

Had the occasion been more propitious, the Count could scarcely have refrained from commenting upon this remarkably republican criticism; but, as it was, he deemed it more advisable to hunt with the hounds.

" That canaille! " he shouted. " Ha, ha! Lord Tulli-wuddle would never so far demean himself! "

" I have it from old Gallosh himself," declared Mr. Maddison.

" And that girl Gallosh told Eleanor the same," added Ri.

" Pooh! " cried the Count. " A mere invention."

" You are certain, sir, that Lord Tulliwuddle gave them no grounds whatever for supposing such a thing? "

" I pledge my reputation as Count of the Austrian Empire, that if my friend be indeed a Tulliwuddle he is faithful to your charming daughter!"

Father and son looked at him shrewdly.

" Being a Tulliwuddle, or any other sort of pampered aristocrat, doesn't altogether guarantee faithfulness," observed the Silver King.

" If he has deceived you, he shall answer to me! " declared the Count. " And between ourselves, as nature's gentleman to nature's gentleman, you may assure Miss

Maddison that there is not the remotest likelihood of this scheming Miss Gallosh ever becoming my friend's bride!"

The two Dariuses were sensibly affected by this assurance.

" As nature's gentleman to nature's gentleman!" repeated the elder with unction, wringing his hand.

His son displayed an equal enthusiasm, and the Count departed with an enhanced reputation and the lingering fragrance of a cocktail upon his tongue.

" Now I think we are in comparatively smooth water," he said to himself as he whizzed back to the castle.

At the door he was received by the butler.

" Mr. Gallosh is waiting for you in the library, my lord," said he, adding confidentially (since the Count had endeared himself to all), "He's terrible impatient for to see your lordship."

EVIDENTLY Mr. Gallosh, while waiting for the Count's return, had so worked up his wrath that it was ready to explode on a hair-trigger touch; and, as evidently, his guest's extreme urbanity made it exceedingly difficult to carry out his threatening intentions.

" I want a word with you, Count. I've been wanting a word with you all morning," he began.

" Believe me, Mr. Gallosh, I appreciate the compliment."

" Where were you ? I mean it was verra annoying not to find you when I wanted you."

The merchant was so evidently divided between anxiety to blurt out his mind while it was yet hot from the making up, and desire not to affront a guest and a man of rank, that the Count could scarcely restrain a smile.

" It is equally annoying to myself. I should have enjoyed a conversation with you at any hour since breakfast."

" Umph," replied his host.

" What can I do for you now? "

Mr. Gallosh looked at him steadfastly.

" Count Bunker," said he, " I am only a plain man "

"The ladies, I assure you, are not of that opinion," interposed the Count politely.

Mr. Gallosh seemed to him to receive this compliment with more suspicion than pleasure.

"I'm saying," he repeated, "that I'm only a plain man of business, and you and your friend are what you'd call swells."

"God forbid that I should!" the Count interjected fervently. "'Toffs,' possibly—but no matter, please continue."

"Well, now, so long as his lordship likes to treat me and my family as kind of belonging to a different sphere, I'm well enough content. I make no pretensions, Count, to be better than what I am."

"I also, Mr. Gallosh, endeavor to affect a similar modesty. It's rather becoming, I think, to a fine-looking man."

"It's becoming to any kind of man that he should know his place. But I was saying, I'd have been content if his lordship had been distant and polite and that kind of thing. But was he? You know yourself, Count, how he's behaved!"

"Perfectly politely, I trust."

"But he's not been what you'd call distant, Count Bunker. In fac', the long and the short of it is just this—what's his intentions towards my Eva?"

"Is it Mrs. Gallosh who desires this information?"

"It is. And myself too; oh, I'm not behindhand where the reputation of my daughters is concerned!"

"Mrs. G. has screwed him up to this," said the Count to himself. Aloud, he asked with his blandest air—

"Was not Lord Tulliwuddle available himself?"

"No; he's gone out."

"Alone?"

"No, not alone."

"In brief, with Miss Gallosh?"

"Quite so; and what'll he be saying to her?"

"He is a man of such varied information that it's hard to guess."

"From all I hear, there's not been much variety so far," said Mr. Gallosh drily.

"Dear me!" observed the Count.

His host looked at him for a few moments.

"Well?" he demanded at length.

"Pardon me if I am stupid, but what comment do you expect me to make?"

"Well, you see, we all know quite well you're more in his lordship's confidence than any one else in the house, and I'd take it as a favor if you'd just give me your honest opinion. Is he just playing himself—or what?"

The worthy Mr. Gallosh was so evidently sincere, and looked at him with such an appealing eye, that the Count found the framing of a suitable reply the hardest task that had yet been set him.

"Mr. Gallosh, if I were in Tulliwuddle's shoes I can only say that I should consider myself a highly fortunate individual; and I do sincerely believe that that is his own conviction also."

"You think so?"

"I do indeed."

Though sensibly relieved, Mr. Gallosh still felt vaguely conscious that if he attempted to repeat this statement for the satisfaction of his wife, he would find it hard to make it sound altogether as reassuring as when accompanied by the Count's sympathetic voice. He ruminated for a minute, and then suddenly recalled what the Count's evasive answers and sympathetic assurances had driven from his mind. Yet it was, in fact, the chief occasion of concern.

" Do you know, Count Bunker, what his lordship has gone and done? "

" Should one inquire too specifically ? " smiled the Count; but Mr. Gallosh remained unmoved.

" You can bear me witness that he told us he was giving this gathering in my Eva's honor ? "

" Undoubtedly."

" Well, he went and told Miss Maddison it was for her sake?"

"Incredible!"

"It's a fact!"

" I refuse to believe my friend guilty of such perfidy! Who told you this?"

" The Maddisons themselves."

" Ha, ha! " laughed the Count, as heartily as he had laughed at Lincoln Lodge; " don't you know these Americans sometimes draw the long bow? "

" You mean to say you don't believe they told the truth?"

" My dear Mr. Gallosh, I would answer you in the oft-quoted words of Horace— 6 Arma virumque cano.' The philosophy of a solar system is sometimes compressed within an eggshell. Say nothing and see!"

He shook his host heartily by the hand as he spoke, and Mr. Gallosh, to his subsequent perplexity, found the interview apparently at a satisfactory conclusion.

" And now," said the Count to himself, " ' Bolt!' is the word."

As he set about his packing in the half-hour that yet remained before luncheon, he was surprised to note that his friend had evidently left no orders yet concerning any preparations for his departure.

" Confound him! I thought he had made up his mind last night! Ah, there he comes—and singing, too, by Jingo! If he wants another day's dalliance "

At this point his reflections were interrupted by the entrance of the jovial Baron himself. He stopped and stared at his friend.

" Vat for do you pack up? "

" Because we leave this afternoon."

" Ach, Bonker, absurd ! To-morrow—yes, to-morrow ve vill leave."

Bunker folded his arms and looked at him seriously.

" I have had two interviews this morning—one with Mr. Maddison, the other with Mr. Gallosh. They were neither of them pleased with you, Baron."

" Not pleased? Vat did zey say? "

Depicting the ire of these gentlemen in the most vivid terms, the Count gave him a summary of his morning's labors.

" Pooh, pooh! Tuts, tuts! " exclaimed the Baron. " I vill make zat all right; never do you fear. Eva, she does smile on me already. Eleanor, she vill also ven I see her. Leave it to me."

" You won't go to-day? "

"To-morrow, Bonker, I swear I vill for certain!"

Bonker pondered.

"Hang it!" he exclaimed. "The worst of it is, I've pledged myself to go upon a visit."

The Baron listened to the tale of his incipient romance with the greatest relish.

"Bot go, my friend! Bot go!" he cried, "and zen come back here to-morrow and ve vill leave to-gezzer."

"Leave you alone, with the barometer falling and the storm-cone hoisted? I don't like to, Baron."

"Bot to leave zat leetle girl—eh, Bonker? How is zat?"

"Was ever a man so torn between two duties!" exclaimed the conscientious Count.

"Ladies come first!" quoth the Baron.

Bunker was obviously strongly tending to this opinion also.

"Can I trust you to guide your own destinies without me?"

The Baron drew himself up with a touch of indignation.

"Am I a child or a fool? I have guided mine destiny vary veil so far, and I zink I can still so do. Ven vill you go to see Miss Wallingford?"

"I'll hire a trap from the village after lunch and be off about four," said the Count. "Long live the ladies! Learn wisdom by my example! Will this tie conquer her, do you think?"

In this befitting spirit he drove off that afternoon, and the Baron, after waving his adieus from the door, strode brimful of confidence towards the drawing-room. His thoughts must have gone astray, for he turned by accident into the wrong room—a small apartment hardly used at all; and before he had time to turn back he stopped petrified at the sight of a picture on the wall. There could be no mistake—it was the original of that ill-omened print he had seen in the Edinburgh hotel, "The Execution of Lord Tulliwuddle." The actual title was there plain to see.

"Zen it vas not a hoax!" he gasped.

His first impulse was to look for a bicycle and tear after the dog-cart.

"But can I ride him in a kilt?" he reflected.

By the time he had fully debated this knotty point his friend was miles upon his way, and the Baron was left ruefully to lament his rashness in parting with such an ally.

CHAPTER XXVII

DURING the horrid period of suspense that followed her visit to Sir Justin, the Baroness von Blitzenberg naturally enough felt disinclined to go much into society, and in fact rarely went out at all during the Baron's absence, except to the houses of one or two of her mother's particular friends. Even then she felt much more inclined to stay at home.

"Need we go to Mrs. Jerwin-Speedy's to-night?" she said one afternoon.

"Certainly," replied the Countess decisively.

Alicia sighed submissively; but this attitude was abruptly changed into one of readiness, nay, even of alacrity, when her mother remarked—

"By the way, she is an aunt of the present Tulli-wuddle. I believe it was you who were asking about him the other day."

"Was I?" said the Baroness carelessly; but she offered no further objections to attending Mrs. Jerwin-Speedy's reception.

She found there a large number of people compressed into a couple of small rooms, and she soon felt so lost in the crush of strangers, and the chances of obtaining any information about Lord Tulliwuddle or his Eva seemed so remote, that she soon began to wish herself comfortably at home again, even though it were only to fret. But fortune, which had so long been unkind to her and indulgent to her erring spouse, chose that night as the turning-point in her tide of favors. Little dreaming how much hung on a mere introduction, Mrs. Jerwin-Speedy led up to the Baroness an apparently nervous and diffident young man.

" Let me introduce my nephew, Lord Tulliwuddle— the Baroness von Blitzenberg," said she; and having innocently hurled this bomb, retired from further participation in the drama.

With young and diffident men Alicia had a pleasant instinct for conducting herself as smilingly as though they were the greatest wits about the town. The envious of her sex declared that it was because she scarcely recognized the difference; but be that as it may, it served her on this occasion in the most admirable stead. She detached the agitated peer from the thickest of the throng, propped him beside her against the wall, and by her kindness at length unloosed his tongue. Then it was she began to suspect that his nervous manner must surely be due to some peculiar circumstance rather than mere constitutional shyness. Made observant by her keen curiosity, she noticed at first a worried, almost hunted, look in his eyes and an extreme impatience of scrutiny by his fellow-guests; but as he gained confidence in her kindness and discretion these passed away, and he appeared simply a garrulous young man, with a tolerably good opinion of himself.

" Poor fellow! He is in trouble of some kind.

Something to do with Eva, of course!" she said to her sympathetically.

The genuine Tulliwuddle had indeed some cause for perturbation. After keeping himself out of the way of all his friends and most of his acquaintances ever since the departure of his substitute, hearing nothing of what was happening at Hechnahoul, and living in daily dread of the ignominious exposure of their plot, he had stumbled by accident against his aunt, explained his prolonged absence from her house with the utmost difficulty, and found himself forced to appease her wounded feelings by appearing where he least wished to be seen—in a crowded London reception-room. No wonder the unfortunate young man seemed nervous and ill at ease.

As for Alicia, she was consumed with anxiety to know why he was here and not in Scotland, as Sir Justin had supposed; and, indeed, to learn a number of things. And now they were rapidly getting on sufficiently familiar terms for her to put a tactful question or two. Encouraged by her sympathy, he began to touch upon his own anxieties.

" A young man ought to get married, I suppose," he remarked confidentially.

The Baroness smiled.

" That depends on whether he likes any one well enough to marry her, doesn't it? "

He sighed.

" Do you think—honestly now," he said solemnly, " that one should marry for love or marry for money ? "

" For love, certainly! "

" You really think so ? You'd advise—er—advise a fellow to blow the prejudices of his friends, and that sort of thing? "

" I should have to know a little more about the case."

He was evidently longing for a confidant.

" Suppose —er—one girl was ripping, but—well— on the stage, for instance."

" On the stage! " exclaimed the Baroness. " Yes, please go on. What about the other girl? "

" Suppose she had simply pots of money, but the fellow didn't know much more about her ? "

" I certainly shouldn't marry a girl I didn't know a good deal about," said the Baroness with conviction.

Lord Tulliwuddle seemed impressed with this opinion.

" That's just what I have begun to think," said he, and gazed down at his pumps with a meditative air.

The Baroness thought the moment had come when she could effect a pretty little surprise.

"Which of them is called Eva?" she asked archly.

To her intense disappointment he merely stared.

" Don't you really know any girl called Eva ? "

He shook his head.

" Can't think of any one."

Suspicion, fear, bewilderment, made her reckless.

" Have you been in Scotland —at your castle, as I heard you were going? "

A mighty change came over the young man. He backed away from her, stammering hurriedly —

" No—yes—I—er—why do you ask me that ? "

"Is there any other Lord Tulliwuddle? " she demanded breathlessly.

He gave her one wild look, and then without so much as a farewell had turned and elbowed his way out of the room.

" It's all up! " he said to himself. " There's no use trying to play that game any longer—Essington has muddled it somehow. Well, I'm free to do what I like now!"

In this state of mind he found himself in the street, hailed the first hansom, and drove headlong from the dangerous regions of Belgravia.

• •••••

Till the middle of the next day the Baroness still managed to keep her own counsel, though she was now so alarmed that she was twenty times on the point of telling everything to her mother. But the arrival of a note from Sir Justin ended her irresolution. It ran thus:

" MY DEAR ALICIA, —I have just learned for certain that Lord T. is at his place in Scotland. Singularly enough, he is described as apparently of foreign extraction, and I hear that he is accompanied by a friend of the name of Count Bunker. I am just setting out for the North myself, and trust that I may be able to elucidate the mystery. Yours very truly,

" JUSTIN WAI/LINGFORD."

" Foreign extraction! Count Bunker ! " gasped the Baroness; and without stopping to debate the matter again, she rushed into her mother's arms, and there sobbed out the strange story of her second letter and the two Lord Tulliwuddles.

It were difficult to say whether anger at her daughter's deceit, indignation with the treacherous Baron, or a stern pleasure in finding her worst prognostications in a fair way to being proved, was the uppermost emotion in Lady Grillyer's mind when she had listened to this relation. Certainly poor Alicia could not but think that sympathy for her troubles formed no ingredient in the mixture.

" To think of your concealing this from me for so long! " she cried; " and Sir Justin abetting you! I shall tell him very plainly what I think of him! But if my daughter sets an example in treachery, what can one expect of one's friends ? "

" After all, mamma, it was my own and Rudolph's concern more than your's! " exclaimed

Alicia, flaring up for an instant.

" Don't answer me, child! " thundered the Countess. " Fetch me a railway time-table, and say nothing that may add to your sin!"

" A time-table, mamma ? What for ? "

" I am going to Scotland," pronounced the Countess.

" Then I shall go too! "

" Indeed you shall not. You will wait here till I have brought Rudolph back to you."

The Baroness said nothing aloud, but within her wounded heart she thought bitterly —

" Mamma seems to forget that even worms will turn sometimes!"

A DECIDEDLY delectable residence," said Count Bunker to himself as his dog-cart approached the lodge gates of The Lash. " And a very proper setting for the pleasant scenes so shortly to be enacted. Lodge, avenue, a bogus turret or two, and a flagstaff on top of 'em — by Gad, I think one may safely assume a tolerable cellar in such a mansion."

As he drove up the avenue between a double line of ancient elms and sycamores, his satisfaction increased and his spirits rose ever higher.

" I wonder if I can forecast the evening: a game of three-handed bridge, in which I trust I'll be lucky enough to lose a little silver, that'll put 'em in good-humor and make old Miss What-d'ye-may-call-her the more willing to go to bed early; then the departure of the chaperon; and then the tete-a-tete! I hope to Heaven I haven't got rusty! "

With considerable satisfaction he ran over the outfit he had brought, deeming it even on second thoughts a singularly happy selection : the dining coat with pale-blue lapels, the white tie of a new material and cut borrowed from the Baron's finery, the socks so ravish-ingly embroidered that he had more than once caught

the ladies at Hechnahoul casting affectionate glances upon them.

" A first-class turn-out," he thought. " And what a lucky thing I thought of borrowing a banjo from young Gallosh ! A coon song in the twilight will break the ground prettily."

By this time they had stopped before the door, and an elderly man - servant, instead of waiting for the Count, came down the steps to meet him. In his manner there was something remarkably sheepish and constrained, and, to the Count's surprise, he thrust forth his hand almost as if he expected it to be shaken. Bunker, though a trifle puzzled, promptly handed him the banjo case, remarking pleasantly—

"My banjo; take care of it, please."

The man started so violently that he all but dropped it upon the steps.

" What the deuce did he think I said ? " wondered the Count. " ' Banjo ' can't have sounded ' dynamite.' "

He entered the house, and found himself in a pleasant hall, where his momentary uneasiness was at once forgotten in the charming welcome of his hostess. Not only she, but her chaperon, received him with a flattering warmth that realized his utmost expectations.

" It was so good of you to come! "«cried Miss Wall-ingford.

" So very kind," murmured Miss Minchell.

" I knew you wouldn't think it too unorthodox! " added Julia.

" I'm afraid orthodoxy is a crime I shall never swing for," said the Count, with his most charming smile.

" I am sure my father wouldn't really mind," said Julia.

" Not if Sir Justin shared your enthusiasm, dear," added Miss Minchell.

" I must teach him to! "

"Good Lord!" thought the Count. "This is friendly indeed."

A few minutes passed in the exchange of these preliminaries, and then his hostess said, with a pretty little air of discipleship that both charmed and slightly puzzled him—

" You do still think that nobody should dine later than six, don't you? I have ordered dinner for six to-night."

" Six! " exclaimed the Count, but recovering himself, added, " An ideal hour—and it is half-past five now. Perhaps I had better think of dressing."

" What you call dressing! " smiled Julia, to his justifiable amazement. " Let me show you to your room."

She led him upstairs, and finally stopped before an open door.

" There!" she said, with an air of pride. " It is really my father's bedroom when he is at home, but I've had it specially prepared for you! Is it just as you would like ? "

Bunker was incapable of observing anything very particularly beyond the fact that the floor was un-carpeted, and as nearly free from furniture as a bedroom floor could well be.

" It is ravishing! " he murmured, and dismissed her with a well-feigned smile.

Bereft even of expletives, he gazed round the apartment prepared for him. It was a few moments before he could bring himself to make a tour of its vast bleakness.

" I suppose that's what they call a truckle-bed," he mused. " Oh, there is one chair—nothing but cold water — towels made of vegetable fibre apparently. The devil take me, is this a reformatory for bogus noblemen!"

He next gazed at the bare whitewashed wall. On it hung one picture—the portrait of a strangely attired man.

" What a shocking-looking fellow!" he exclaimed, and went up to examine it more closely.

Then, with a stupefying shock, he read this legend beneath it—

" Count Bunker. Philosopher, teacher, and martyr."

For a minute he stared in rapt amazement, and then sharply rang the bell.

" Hang it," he said to himself, " I must throw a little light on this somehow ! "

Presently the elderly man - servant appeared, this time in a state of still more obvious confusion. For a moment he stared at the Count —who was too discomposed by his manner to open his lips—and then, once more stretching out his hand, exclaimed in a choked voice and a strong Scotch accent—

" How are ye, Bunker! "

" What the deuce!" shouted the Count, evading the proffered hand-shake with an agile leap.

The poor fellow turned scarlet, and in an humble voice blurted out—

" She told me to do it! Miss Julia said ye'd like me to shake hands and just ca' ye plain Bunker. I beg your pardon, sir; oh, I beg your pardon humbly! "

The Count looked at him keenly.

" He is evidently telling the truth," he thought.

Thereupon he took from his pocket half a sovereign.

" My good fellow," he began. " By the way, what's your name? "

" Mackenzie, SIT."

"Mackenzie, my honest friend, I clearly perceive that Miss Wallingford, in her very kind efforts to gratify my unconventional tastes, has put herself to quite unnecessary trouble. She has even succeeded in surprising me, and I should be greatly obliged if you would kindly explain to me the reasons for her conduct, so far as you can."

At this point the half-sovereign changed hands.

"In the first place," resumed the Count, "what is the meaning of this remarkably villainous portrait labelled with my name?"

"That, sir," stammered Mackenzie, greatly taken aback by the inquiry. "Why, sir, that's the famous Count Bunker—your uncle, sir, is he no'?"

Bunker began to see a glimmer of light, though the vista it illumined was scarcely a much pleasanter prospect than the previous bank of fog. He remembered now, for the first time since his journey north, that the Baron, in dubbing him Count Bunker, had encouraged him to take the title on the ground that it was a real dignity once borne by a famous personage; and in a flash he realized the pitfalls that awaited a solitary false step.

"That my uncle!" he exclaimed with an air of pleased surprise, examining the portrait more attentively; "by Gad, I suppose it is! But I can't say it is a flattering likeness. * Philosopher, teacher, and martyr'—how apt a description! I hadn't noticed that before, or I should have known at once who it was."

Still Mackenzie was looking at him with a perplexed and uneasy air.

"Miss Wallingford, sir, seems under the impression that you would be wanting jist the same kind of things as he likit," he remarked diffidently.

The Count laughed.

"Hence the condemned cell she's put me in? I see! Ha, ha! No, Mackenzie, I have moved with the times. In fact, my uncle's philosophy and teachings always struck me as hardly suitable for a gentleman."

"I was thinking that mysel'," observed Mackenzie.

"Well, you understand now how things are, don't you? By the way, you haven't put out my evening clothes, I notice."

"You werena to dress, sir, Miss Julia said."

"Not to dress! What the deuce does she expect me to dine in?"

With a sheepish grin Mackenzie pointed to something upon the bed which the Count had hitherto taken to be a rough species of quilt.

"She said you might like to wear that, sir."

The Count took it up.

"It appears to be a dressing-gown!" said he.

"She said, sir, your uncle was wont to dine in it."

"Ah! It's one of my poor uncle's eccentricities, is it? Very nice of Miss Wallingford; but all the same I think you can put out my evening clothes for me; and, I say, get me some hot water and a couple of towels that feel a little less like sandpaper, will you? By the way—one moment, Mackenzie!—you needn't mention anything of this to Miss Wallingford. I'll explain it all to her myself."

It is remarkable how the presence or absence of a few of the very minor accessories of life will affect the humor even of a man so essentially philosophical as Count Bunker. His equanimity was most marvelously restored by a single jugful of hot water, and by the time he came to survey his blue lapels in the mirror the completest confidence shone in his humorous eyes.

"How deuced pleased she'll be to find I'm a white man after all," he reflected. " Supposing I'd really turned out a replica of that unshaved heathen on the wall—poor girl, what a dull evening she'd have spent!

Perhaps I'd better break the news gently for the chaperon's sake, but once we get her off to bed I rather fancy the fair Julia and I will smile together over my dear uncle's dressing-gown! "

And in this humor he strode forth to conquer.

COUNT BUNKER could not but observe that Miss Wallingford's eyes expressed more surprise than pleasure when he entered the drawing-room, and he was confirmed in his resolution to let his true character appear but gradually. Afterwards he could not congratulate himself too heartily on this prudent decision.

" I fear," he said, " that I am late." (It was in fact half-past six by now.) " I have been searching through my wardrobe to find some nether garments at all appropriate to the overall—if I may so term it— which you were kind enough to lay out for me. But I found mustard of that particular shade so hard to match that I finally decided in favor of this more conventional habit. I trust you don't mind ? "

Both the ladies, though evidently disappointed, excused him with much kindness, and Miss Minchell alluded directly to his blue lapels as evidence that even now he held himself somewhat aloof from strict orthodoxy.

" May we see any allusion to your uncle, the late Count Bunker, in his choice of color? " she asked in a reverently hushed voice.

" Yes," replied the Count readily; " my aunt's stockings were of that hue."

From the startled glances of the two ladies it became plain that the late Count Bunker had died a bachelor.

" My other aunt," he exclaimed unabashed; yet nevertheless it was with decided pleasure that he heard dinner announced immediately afterwards.

" They seem to know something about my uncle," he said to himself. " I must glean a few particulars too."

A horrible fear lest his namesake might have dined solely upon herbs, and himself be expected to follow his example, was pleasantly dissipated by a glance at the menu; but he confessed to a sinking of his heart when he observed merely a tumbler beside his own plate and a large brown jug before him.

" Good heavens! " he thought, " do they imagine an Austrian count is necessarily a beer drinker ? "

With a sigh he could not quite smother, he began to pour the contents into his glass, and then set it down abruptly, emitting a startled exclamation.

" What is the matter ? " cried Julia sympathetically.

Her eyes (he was embarrassed to note) followed his every movement like a dog's, and her apprehension clearly was extreme.

" This seems to be water," smiled the Count, with an effort to carry off their error as pleasantly for them as possible.

" Isn't it good water ? " asked Julia with an air of concern.

It was the Count's turn to open his eyes.

" You have concluded then that I am a teetotaler? "

" Of course, we know you are! "

" If we may judge by your prefaces," smiled Miss Minchell.

The Count began to realize the hazards that beset him; but his spirit stoutly rose to meet the shock of the occasion.

" There is no use in attempting to conceal my idiosyncrasies, I see," he answered. " But to-night, will you forgive me if I break through the cardinal rule of my life and ask you for a little stimulant? My doctor "

" I see! " cried Miss Wallingford compassionately. " Of course, one can't dispute a doctor's orders. What would you like? "

" Oh, anything you have. He did recommend champagne—if it was good; but anything will do."

" A bottle of the very best champagne, Mackenzie! "

The dinner now became an entirely satisfactory meal. Inspired by his champagne and by the success of his audacity in so easily surmounting all difficulties, the Count delighted his hostesses by the vivacity and originality of his conversation. On the one hand, he chose topics not too flippant in themselves and treated them with a becomingly serious air; on the other, he carefully steered the talk away from the neighborhood of his uncle.

" By the time I fetch out my banjo they'll have forgotten all about him," he said to himself complacently.

Knowing well the importance of the individual factor in all the contingencies of life, he set himself, in the meanwhile, to study with some attention the two ladies beside him. Miss Minchell he had already summarized as an agreeable nonentity, and this impression was only confirmed on better acquaintance. It was quite evident, he perceived, that she was dragged practically unresisting in Miss Wallingford's wake—even to the length of abetting the visit of an unknown bachelor in the absence of Miss Wallingford's parent.

As for Julia, he decided that she was even better-looking and more agreeable than he had at first imagined; though, having the gayest of hearts himself, he was a trifle disconcerted to observe the uniform seriousness of her ideas. How one could reconcile her ecstatic enthusiasm for the ideal with her evident devotion to himself he was at a loss to conceive.

" However, we will investigate that later," he thought.

But first came a more urgent question: Had his uncle and his " prefaces " committed him to forswear tobacco? He resolved to take the bull by the horns.

" I hope you will not be scandalized to learn that I have acquired the pernicious habit of smoking ? " he said as they rose from the table.

" I told you he was smoking a cigar at Hechnahoul! " cried Miss Minchell with an air of triumph.

" I thought you were mistaken," said Julia, and the Count could see that he had slipped a little from his pedestal.

This must not be permitted; yet he must smoke.

" Of course I don't smoke real tobacco ! " he exclaimed.

" Oh, in that case," cried Julia, " certainly then you may smoke in the drawing-room. What is it you use? "

" A kind of herb that subdues the appetites, Miss Wallingford."

He could see at a glance that he was more firmly on his pedestal than ever.

CHAPTER XXX

"I HAVE been longing for this moment!" said Julia softly. The Count and she were seated over the drawing-room fire, Bunker in an easy-chair, smoking one of the excellent cigars which he had so grievously slandered, Julia upon a stool by his knees, her face suffused with the most intense expression of rapture. Miss Minchell was in the background, shrouded in shadow, purporting to be enjoying a nap; yet the Count could not but think that in so large a house a separate apartment might well have been provided for her. Her presence, he felt, circumscribed his actions uncomfortably.

" So have I !" he murmured, deeming this the most appropriate answer.

" Now we can talk about him! " He started, but preserved his composure. " Couldn't we keep him till morning? " he suggested. " But that is why you are here! " She spoke as if this were self-evident; while the Count read himself a thousand lessons upon the errors vanity is apt to lead one into. Yet his politeness remained unruffled

" Of course," he answered. " Of course ! But you see my knowledge of him "

He was about to say that it was very slight, when, fortunately for him, she interrupted with an eager—

" I know! I know! You were more than a son to him!"

" The deuce and all! " thought the Count. " That was a narrow squeak! "

" Do you know," she continued in the same tone, " I have actually had the audacity to translate one of his books—your preface and all."

" I understand the allusion now," thought Bunker.

Aloud he had the presence of mind to inquire—

"Which was it?"

" ' Existence Seriously Reviewed.' "

" You couldn't have made a better choice," he assured her.

"And now, what can you tell me about him? " she cried.

" Suppose we talk about the book instead," suggested Bunker, choosing what seemed the lesser of two evils.

"Oh, do!"

She rose impetuously, brought with a reverent air a beautifully written and neatly tied-up manuscript, and sat again by his knee. Looking over his shoulder he could see that the chaperon was wide awake and prepared to listen rapturously also.

" I have so often longed to have some one with me who could explain things—the very deep things, you know.

But to think of having you—the Editor and nephew! It's too good to be true."

" Only eight o'clock," he said to himself, glancing at the clock. " I'm in for a night of it."

The vision of a game of bridge and a coon song on the banjo from that moment faded quite away, and the Count even tucked his feet as far out of sight as possible, since those entrancing socks served to remind him too poignantly of what might have been.

" What exactly did he mean by this ? " began Julia, "'Let Potentates fear! Let Dives tremble! The horny hand of the poor Man in the Street is stretched forth to grasp his birthright!' "

"For 'birthright' read 'pocket-book.' There's a mistake in the translation," he answered promptly. " It appears to be an indirect argument for an increase in the Metropolitan police."

"Are you sure? I thought—surely it alludes to Socialism!"

"Of course; and the best advertisement for Socialism is a collision with the bobbies. My uncle was a remarkably subtle man, I assure you."

"How very ingenious!" exclaimed Miss Minchell from the background.

Julia did her best to feel convinced; but it was in a distinctly less ecstatic voice that she read her next extract.

"'Alcohol, riches, and starched linen are the moths and worms of society.' I suppose he means that they eat away its foundations?"

"On the contrary, he was an enthusiastic entomologist. He merely meant to imply that it isn't every one who can appreciate a glass of port and a clean shirt."

"But he didn't appreciate those things himself!"

"No; poor fellow. He often wished he could, though."

"Did he really?"

"Oh, you've no idea how tired he grew of flannel and ginger-beer! Many a time he's said to me, 'My boy, learn to take what's set before you, even at an alderman's table.' Ah, his was a generous creed, Miss Wallingford!"

"Yes, I suppose it was," said Julia submissively.

His advantage in being able to claim an intimate personal knowledge of the late philosopher's tastes encouraged the Count greatly. Realizing that a nephew could not well be contradicted, he was emboldened to ask whether there were any more points on which his authority could be of assistance.

"Oh yes," said she, "only—only somehow you seem to throw a different light on everything."

"Naturally, dear," chimed in Miss Minchell, "a personal explanation always makes things seem different."

Julia sighed, but summed up her courage to read out—

"'When woman is prized according to her intellect and man according to his virtue; oh, then mankind will return to Eden!'"

COUNT BUNKER

"That," said he, "is one of the rare instances of my uncle's pessimism."

"Of his pessimism! How can you say that?"

"He meant to imply that mankind would have to wait for some considerable time. But do not feel dismayed. My own opinion is that so long as woman is fair and man has the wit to appreciate her, we are in Eden."

The gracious tone in which he delivered this dictum, and the moving smile that accompanied it, appeared to atone completely for his relative's cynical philosophy. With a smile and a sigh Julia murmured—

"Do you really think so?"

"I do," said the Count fervently; "and now suppose we were to have a little music?"

"Oh yes!" cried Miss Minchell; "do you perform, Count Bunker?"

"I sometimes sing a little to the guitar."

"To the guitar!" said Julia. "How delicious! Have you brought it?"

"I have been so bold," he smiled, and promptly went to fetch this instrument.

In a few minutes he returned with an apologetic air.

"I find that by some error they have sent me away with a banjo instead," he exclaimed. "But I dare say I could manage an accompaniment on that if you would condescend to listen to me."

He felt so exceedingly disinclined for expounding a philosophy any longer that he gave them no time to dissent, even had they wished to, but on the instant struck up that pathetic ditty—

" Down by whar de beans grow blue. "

And no sooner had he finished it than (barely waiting for his meed of applause) he further regaled them with—

« Twould make a fellow Turn green and yellow ! "

Finally, as a tit-bit, he contributed—•,

ts When hubby's gone to Brighton, And I've sent the cook to bed, Oh who's that a-knocking on the window ! "

At the conclusion of this concert he knew not whether to feel more relieved or chagrined to observe that his fair hostess had her eyes fixed upon the clock. Thanking him with a slightly embarrassed air, she threw a pointed glance at Miss Minchell, and the two ladies rose.

" I am afraid you will think we keep very early hours," she began.

" It is one of the best rules in my uncle's philosophy," he interposed.

Yet though glad enough to have come so triumphantly to the end of his ordeal, he could not bring himself to let his charming disciple leave him in a wounded or even disappointed mood. As soon as Miss Minchell had passed through the door he quietly laid his hand upon Julia's arm, and with a gesture beckoned her back into the room.

" Pardon my seeming levity, Miss Wallingford,"
COUNT BUNKER
he said in a grave and gentle voice, " but you know not what emotions I had to contend with! I thank you for your charming sympathy, and I beg you to accept in my uncle's name that salute by which his followers distinguish the faithful."

And he thereupon kissed the blushing girl with a heartiness that restored her confidence in him completely.

" Well," he said to himself as he retired with his candle, " I've managed to get a fair penn'orth out of it after all."

IN spite of the Spartan transformation which Sir Justin's bedroom had undergone, our adventurer enjoyed an excellent night's rest. So fast asleep was he at the hour of eight next morning that it took him a few seconds to awake to the full possession of his faculties, even when disturbed by a loud exclamation at his bedside. He then became aware of the presence of an entire stranger in his room—a tall and elderly man, with a long nose and a grizzled beard. This intruder had apparently just drawn up the blind, and was now looking about him with an expression of the greatest concern.

" Mackenzie! " he cried, in the voice of one accustomed to be heard with submission, " What have you been doing to my room ? "

The butler, too confused for coherent speech, was in the act of bringing in a small portmanteau.

" I —I mentioned, Sir Justin, your room was hardly ready for ye, sir. Perhaps, sir, if ye'd come into the pink room "

" What the deuce, there's hardly a stick of furniture left! And whose clothes are these ? "

" Mine," answered the Count suavely.

The stranger started violently, and turned upon the

bed an eye at first alarmed, then rapidly becoming lit with indignation.

"Who—who is this?" he shouted.

" That, sir—that " stammered Mackenzie.

" Is Count Bunker," said the Count, who remained entirely courteous in spite of the inconvenience of this intrusion. " Have I the pleasure of addressing Sir Justin Wallingford? "

" You have, sir."

" In that case, Mackenzie will be able to give you a satisfactory account of my presence; and in half an hour or so I shall have the pleasure of joining you downstairs."

The Count, with a polite smile, turned over in bed, as though to indicate that the interview was now at an end. But his visitor apparently had other views.

" I should be obliged by some explanation from yourself of your entry into my house," said he, steadily keeping his eye upon the Count.

" Now how the deuce shall I get out of this hole without letting Julia into another? " wondered Bunker; but before he could speak, Mackenzie had blurted out—

" Miss Wallingford, sir—the gentleman is a friend of hers, sir."

" What! " thundered Sir Justin.

" I assure you that Miss Wallingford was actuated by the highest motives in honoring me with an invitation to The Lash," said Bunker earnestly.

He had already dismissed an ingenious account of himself as a belated wanderer, detained by stress of

weather, as certain to be contradicted by Julia herself, and decided instead on risking all upon his supposed uncle's saintly reputation.

" How came she to invite you, sir? " demanded Sir Justin.

" As my uncle's nephew, merely."

Sir Justin stared at him in silence, while he brought the full force of his capacious mind to bear upon the situation.

"Your name, you say, is Bunker?" he observed at length.

" Count Bunker," corrected that nobleman.

" Ah! Doubtless, then, you are the same gentleman who has been residing with Lord Tulliwuddle? "

" I am unaware of a duplicate."

" And the uncle you allude to ? "

By a wave of his hand the Count referred him to the portrait upon the wall. Sir Justin now stared at it.

" Bunker—Count Bunker," he repeated in a musing tone, and then turned to the present holder of that dignity with a look in his eye which the adventurer disliked exceedingly.

" I will confer with you later," he observed. " Mackenzie, remove my portmanteau."

In a voice inaudible to the Count he gave another order, which was followed by Mackenzie also removing the Count's clothes from their chair.

" I say, Mackenzie!" expostulated Bunker, now beginning to feel seriously uneasy; but heedless of his protest the butler hastened with them from the room.

Then, with a grim smile and a surprising alacrity of movement, Sir Justin changed the key into the outside of the lock, passed through the door, and shut and locked it behind him.

"The devil!" ejaculated Count Bunker.

Here was a pretty predicament! And the most ominous feature about it appeared to him to be the deliberation with which his captor had acted. It seemed that he had got himself into a worse scrape than he could estimate.

He wasted no time in examining his prison with an eye to the possibility of an escape, but it became very quickly evident that he was securely trapped. From the windows he could not see even a water-pipe within hail, and the door was unburstably ponderous. Besides, a gentleman attired either in pajamas or evening dress will naturally shrink from flight across country at nine o'clock in the morning. It seemed to the Count that he was as well in bed as anywhere else, and upon this opinion he acted.

In about an hour's time the door was cautiously unlocked, and a tray, containing some breakfast, laid upon the floor ; but at the same time he was permitted to see that a cordon of grooms and keepers guarded against his flight. He showed a wonderful appetite, all circumstances considered, smoked a couple of cigars, and at last decided upon getting up and donning his evening clothes. Thereafter nothing occurred, beyond the arrival of a luncheon tray, till the afternoon was well advanced; by which time even his good spirits had become a trifle damped, and his apprehensions considerably increased.

At last his prison door was again thrown open, this time by Sir Justin himself.

" Come in, my dear," he said in a grave voice; and with a downcast eye and scarlet cheek the fair Julia met her guest again.

Her father closed the door, and they seated themselves before their prisoner, who, after a profound obeisance to the lady, faced them from the edge of his bed with an air of more composure than he felt.

" I await your explanation, Sir Justin," he began, striking at once the note which seemed to him (so far as he could guess) most likely to be characteristic of an innocent and much-injured man.

" You shall have it," said Sir Justin grimly. " Julia, you asked this person to my house under the impression that he was the nephew of that particularly obnoxious fanatic, Count Herbrand Bunker, and still engaged upon furthering his relative's philanthropic and other visionary schemes."

" But isn't he " began Julia with startled eyes.

" I am Count Bunker," said our hero firmly.

" The nephew in question ? " inquired Sir Justin.

" Certainly, sir."

Again Sir Justin turned to his daughter.

" I have already told you what I think of your conduct under any circumstances. What your feelings will be I can only surmise when I inform you that I have detained this adventurer here until I had time to despatch a wire and receive an answer from Scotland Yard."

Both Count and Julia started.

" What, sir! " exclaimed Bunker.

Quite unmoved by his protest, his captor continued, this time addressing him—

" My memory, fortunately, is unusually excellent, and when you told me this morning who you were related to, I recalled at once something I had heard of your past career. It is now confirmed by the reply I received to my telegram."

" And what, Sir Justin, does Scotland Yard have to say about me ? "

" Julia," said her parent, " this unhappy young man did indeed profess for some time a regard for his uncle's teachings, and even, I believe, advocated them in writing. In this way he obtained the disposal of considerable funds contributed by unsuspicious persons for ostensibly philanthropic purposes. About two years ago these funds and Count Bunker simultaneously disappeared, and your estimable guest was last heard of under an assumed name in the republic of Uruguay."

Uncomfortable as his predicament was, this picture of himself as the fraudulent philanthropist was too much for Bunker's sense of humor, and to the extreme astonishment of his visitors he went off into a fit of laughter so hearty and prolonged that it was some time before he recovered his gravity.

" My dear friends," he exclaimed at last, " I am not that Bunker at all! In fact I was only created a few

weeks ago. Bring me back my clothes, and in return I'll tell you a deuced sight funnier story even than that."

Sir Justin rose and led his daughter to the door.

" You will have an opportunity to-morrow," he replied stiffly. " In the meantime I shall leave you to the enjoyment of the joke."

" But, my dear sir "

Sir Justin turned his back, and the door closed upon him again.

Count Bunker's position was now less supportable than ever.

" Escape I must," he thought.

And hardly had he breathed the word when a gleam of his old luck seemed to return. He was standing by the window, and presently he observed a groom ride up on a bicycle, dismount, and push it through an outhouse door. Then the man strolled off, and he said to himself, with an uprising of his spirits—

" There's my steed—if I could once get to it! "

Then again he thought the situation over, and gradually the prospect of a midnight ride on a bicycle over a road he had only once traversed, clad in his emblazoned socks and blue-lapelled coat, appeared rather less entertaining than another night's confinement. So he lit his last cigar, threw himself on the bed, and resigned himself to the consolations of an innocent heart and a practical philosophy.

CHAPTER XXXII

THE clearness of the Count's conscience may be gauged when it is narrated that no sooner had he dismissed the stump of his cigar toward the grate than he dropped into a peaceful doze and remained placidly unconscious of his perils for the space of an hour or more. He was then awakened by the sound of a key being gently turned, and his opening eyes rested upon a charming vision of Julia Wallingford framed in the outline of the door.

" Hush! " she whispered; " I —I have brought a note for you!"

Smoothing his hair as he met her, the Count thanked her with an air of considerable feeling, and took from her hand a twisted slip of paper.

" It was brought by a messenger—a man in a kilt, who came in a motor car. I didn't know whether father would let you have it, so I brought it up myself."

" Is the messenger waiting? "

" No; he went straight off again."

Unrolling the scrap he read this brief message scrawled in pencil and evidently in dire haste—

" All is lost ! I am prisoner! Go straightway to London for help from my Embassy.

"Good heavens!" he exclaimed aloud.

"Is it bad news?" asked Julia, with a solicitude that instantly suggested possibilities to his fertile brain.

"Horribly!" he said. "It tells of a calamity that has befallen a very dear friend of mine! Oh, Rudolph, Rudolph! And I a helpless prisoner!"

As he anticipated, this outburst of emotion was not without its effect.

"I am so sorry!" she said. "I— I don't believe, Count Bunker, you are as guilty as father says!"

"I swear to you I am not!"

"Can I—help you?"

He thought swiftly.

"Is there any one about the house just now?"

"Oh yes; the keeper is stationed in the hall!"

"Miss Wallingford, if you would atone for a deep injury which you have inadvertently done an innocent man, bring me fifty feet of stout rope! And, I say, see that the door of the bicycle house is left unlocked. Will you do this?"

"I—I'll try."

A sound on the stairs alarmed her, and with a fleeting smile of sympathy she was gone and the door locked upon him again.

Again the time passed slowly by, and he was left to ponder over the critical nature of the situation as revealed by the luckless Baron's intelligence. Clearly he must escape to-night, at all hazards.

"What's that? My rope?" he wondered.

But it was only the arrival of his dinner, brought as before upon a tray and set just within the door, as though they feared for the bearer's life should he venture within reach of this desperate adventurer from Uruguay.

"A very large dish for a very small appetite," he thought, as he bore his meal over to the bed and drew his chair up before it.

It looked indeed as though a roasted goose must be beneath the cover. He raised it, and there, behold! lay a large coil of excellent new rope. The Count chuckled.

"Commend me to the heart and the wit of women! What man would ever have provided so dainty a dish as this? Unless, indeed" (he had the breadth of mind to add) "it happened to be a charming adventuress who was in trouble."

Drinking the half pint of moderate claret which they had allowed him to the happiness and prosperity of all true-hearted women, he could not help regretting that his imprisoned confederate should be so unlikely to enjoy similar good fortune.

"He went too far with those two dear girls. A woman deceived as he has deceived them will never forgive him. They'd stand sentry at his cell-door sooner than let the poor Baron escape," he reflected com-miserately, and sighed to think of the disastrous effect this mishap might have both upon his friend's diplomatic career and domestic felicity.

While waiting for the dusk to deepen, and endeavoring to console himself for the lack of cigars with the poor remedy of cigarettes, he employed his time profitably in tying a series of double knots upon the line of rope. Then at last, when he could see the stars bright above the trees and hear no sound in the house, he pulled his bed softly to the open window, and to it fastened one end of his rope securely. The other he quietly let drop, and losing not an instant followed it hand under hand, murmuring anathemas on the rough wall that so scraped his evening trousers.

On tiptoe he stole to the door through which the bicycle had gone. It yielded to a push, and once inside he ventured to strike a match.

" By Gad! I've a choice of half a dozen," he exclaimed.

It need scarcely be said that he selected the best; and after slitting with his pocket-knife the tires of all the others, he mounted and pedalled quietly down the drive. The lodge gates stood open; the road, a trifle muddy but clear of all traffic, stretched visible for a long way in the starlight; the breeze blew fair behind him.

" May Providence guide me to the station," he prayed, and rode off into the night.

CHAPTER XXXIII

SUPPOSE the clock be set back four-and-twenty hours, and behold now the Baron von Blitzen-berg, the diplomatist and premier baron of Bavaria, engaged in unhappy argument with himself. Unhappy, because his reason, though so carefully trained from the kindergarten upward, proved unable to combat the dismal onsets of superstition.

"Pooh! who cares for an old picture?" Reason would reiterate.

" It is an omen," said Superstition simply; and Reason stood convicted as an empty braggart.

But if Time be the great healer, Dinner is at least a clever quack, and when he and old Mr. Rentoul had consumed well-nigh a bottle and a half of their host's port between them, the outlook became much less gloomy. A particularly hilarious evening in the drawing-room completed the triumph of mind over what he was now able to term " jost nonsense," and he slept that night as soundly as the Count was simultaneously slumbering in Sir Justin's bed-room. And there was no unpleasant awakening in the Baron's case. On the contrary, all nature seemed in a conspiracy to make the last day of his adventure pleasant. The sun shone brightly, his razors had an excellent edge, sausages were served for breakfast, and when he joined the family afterwards he found them as affectionately kind as a circle of relations. In fact, the Baron had dropped more than one hint the night before of such a nature that they had some reason for supposing relationship imminent. It is true Eva was a little disappointed that the actual words were not yet said, and when he made an airy reference to paying a farewell call that morning upon their neighbors at Lincoln Lodge, she exhibited so much disapproval in her air that he said at once—

"Ach, veil, I shall jost go after lonch and be back in an hour and a half. I jost vish to say good-bye, zat is all."

Little guessing how much was to hang upon this postponement, he drove over after luncheon with a mind entirely reassured. With only an afternoon to be safely passed, no mishap, he was sure, could possibly happen now. If indeed the Maddisons chose to be offended with him, why, then, his call would merely be the briefer and he would recommend Eva for the post of Lady Tulliwuddle without qualification. It was his critics who had reason to fear, not he.

Miss Maddison was at home, the staff of footmen assured him, and, holding his head as high as a chieftain should, he strode into her sanctuary.

"Do I disturb you?"

He asked this with a quicker beating heart. Not Eleanor alone, but her father and Hi confronted him, and it was very plain to see that a tempest was in the

brewing. Her eyes were bright with tears and indignation; their brows heavy with formidable frowns. At the first moment of his entering, extreme astonishment at seeing him was clearly their dominant emotion, and as evidently it rapidly developed into a sentiment even less hospitable.

"Why, this beats the devil!" ejaculated Mr. Mad-dison; and for a moment this was the sole response to his inquiry.

The next to speak was Ri—

" Show it him, Poppa! Confront him with the evidence! "

With ominous deliberation the millionaire picked up a newspaper from the floor, where apparently it had been crumpled and flung, smoothed out the creases, and approached the Baron till their noses were in danger of collision. While executing this manoeuvre the silence was only broken by the suppressed sobbing of his daughter. Then at last he spoke.

" Our mails, sir, have just arrived. This, sir, is ' The Times ' newspaper, published in the city of London yesterday morning."

He shook it in the Baron's face with a sudden vehemence that caused that nobleman to execute an abrupt movement backward.

" Take it," continued the millionaire—" take it, sir, and explain this if you can!"

So confused had the Baron's mind become already that it was with difficulty he could decipher the following petrifying announcement —

" Tulliwuddle—Herringay.—In London, privately, Lord Tulliwuddle to Constance, daughter of Robert Herringay."

The Baron's brain reeled.

" Here is another paragraph that may interest you," pursued Mr. Maddison, turning the paper outside in with an alarmingly vigorous movement, and presenting a short paragraph for the Baron's inspection. This ran—

"PEER AND ACTRESS.

" As announced in our marriage column, the wedding took place yesterday, privately, of Lord Tulliwuddle, kinsman and heir of the late peer of that name, so well known in London and Scottish society, and Miss Constance Herringay, better known as ' Connie Fitz Au-byn,' of the Gaiety Theatre. It is understood that the young couple have departed for the Mediterranean."

In a few seconds given him to prepare his mind, the Baron desperately endeavored to imagine what the resourceful Bunker would say or do under these awful circumstances.

"Well, sir?" said Mr. Maddison.

"It is a lie!"

"A lie?"

Ri laughed scornfully.

" Mean to say no such marriage took place? "

" It vas not me."

"Who was it, then?"

" Anozzer man, perhaps."

"Another Lord Tulliwuddle? " inquired the millionaire.

" Zey have made a mistake mit ze name. Yes, zat is how."

"Can it be possible?" cried Eleanor eagerly, her grief for the moment forgotten.

"No," said her father; "it is not possible. The announcement is confirmed by the paragraph. A mistake is inconceivable."

The Baron thought he perceived a brilliant idea.

" Ach, it is ze ozzer Tollvoddle!" he exclaimed. " So! zat is it, of course."

" You mean to say there is another peerage of Tulliwuddle?"

" Oh, yes."

"Fetch Debrett, Hi!"

But Ri had already not only fetched Debrett, but found the place.

" A darned lie. Thought so," he observed succinctly.

The luckless diplomatist was now committed to perdition.

" It is not in ze books," he exclaimed. " It is bot a baronetcy."

"A baronetcy!"

" And illegitimate also."

" Sir," burst forth Ri, " you are a thundering liar! Is this your marriage notice ? "

The Baron changed his tactics.

"Yes! "he declared.

Eleanor screamed.

" Don't fuss, Eleanor," said her father kindly. " That ain't true, anyhow. Why, the day before yesterday he was throwing that darned hammer."

" Which came down last night in our yard with the head burst! " added Ri contemptuously. " Found you out there too! "

" Is that so! " exclaimed his father.

"That is so, sir!"

The three looked at him, and it was hard to say whether indignation or contempt was more prominent in their faces. This was more than he could endure.

" I vill not be so looked at!" he cried; " I viU leave you!"

" No you won't! " said Ri.

And the Baron saw his retreat cut off by the athletic and determined young man.

" Before you leave, we have one or two questions to ask you," said Mr. Maddison. " Are you Lord Tulli-wuddle, or are you not ? "

" Yes!—No! " replied the Baron.

"Which, sir?"

Expanding his chest, he made the awe-inspiring announcement—

" I am moch greater zan Tollyvoddle! I am ze Baron Rudolph von Blitzenberg!"

" Another darned lie! " commented Ri.

Mr. Maddison laughed sardonically; while Eleanor, with flashing eyes, now joined in the attack upon the hapless nobleman.

COUNT BUNKER

" You wretched creature! Isn't it enough to have shammed to be one peer without shamming to be another? "

" Bot I am! Ja, I swear to you! Can you not see zat I am noble ? "

" Curiously enough we can't," replied Mr. Maddison.

But his daughter's scepticism was a little shaken by the fervor of his assurances.

" But, Poppa, perhaps he may be a German peer."

" German waiter, more likely! " sneered Ri. " What shall we do with him? Tar and feathers, I guess, would just about suit his complaint."

" No, Ri, no," said his father cautiously. " Remember we are no longer beneath the banner of freedom. In this benighted country it might lead into trouble. Guess we can find him accommodation, though, in that bit of genuine antique above the harness-room. It's fitted with a very substantial lock. We'll make Dugald M'Culloch responsible for this Baron till the police take him over."

Vain were the Baron's protests; and upon the appearance of Dugald M'Culloch, fisherman and factotum to the millionaire, accompanied by three burly satellites, vain, he perceived, would be the most desperate resistance. He plead the privileges of a foreign diplomatist, threatened a descent of the German army upon Lincoln Lodge, guaranteed an intimate acquaintance with the American ambassador—" Who vill make you sorry for zis ! " but all without moving Mr. Maddison's resolution. Even Eleanor whispered a word for

COUNT BUNKER

him and was repulsed, for he overheard her father replying to her—

" No, no, Eleanor; no more a diplomatist than you would have been Lady Tulliwuddle. Guess I know what I'm doing."

Whereupon the late Lord Tulliwuddle, kilt and all, was conveyed by a guard of six tall men and deposited in the bit of genuine antique above the harness-room. This proved to be a small chamber in a thick-walled wing of the original house, now part of the back premises; and there, with his face buried in his hands, the poor prisoner moaned aloud—

" Oh, my life, she is geblasted! I am undone! Oh, I am lost!"

" Will it be so bad as that, indeed? "

He looked up with a start, and perceived Dugald, his jailor, gazing upon him with an expression of indescribable sagacity.

" The master will be sending me with his car to tell the folks at Hechnahoul," added Dugald.

Still the Baron failed to comprehend the exchange of favors suggested by his jailor's sympathetic voice.

" Go, zen!" he muttered, and bent his head.

" You will not be wishing to send no messages to your friends ? "

At last the prisoner understood. For a sovereign Dugald promised to convey a note to the Count; for five he undertook to bribe the chauffeur to convey him to The Lash, when he learned where that gentleman

was to be found. And lie further decided to be faithful to his trust, since, as he prudently reflected—

" If he will be a real chentleman after all it shall not be well to be hard with him. And if he will not be, nobody shall know."

The Baron felt a trifle less hopeless now, yet so black did the prospect remain that he firmly believed he should never be able to raise his head again and meet the gaze of his fellow-men; not at least if he stayed in that room till the police arrived.

NOT even the news of Flodden brought direr dismay to Hechnahoul than Mr. Maddison's brief note. Lord Tulliwuddle an impostor? That magnificent young man a fraud? So much geniality, brawn, and taste for the bagpipes merely the sheep's clothing that hid a wandering wolf? Incredible! Yet, on second thoughts, how very much more thrilling than if he had really been an ordinary peer! And what a judgment on the presumption of Mr. and Mrs. Gallosh! Hard luck on Eva, of course —but, then, girls who aspire to marry out of their own station must expect this kind of thing.

The latter part of this commentary was naturally not that of the pretender's host and hostess. In the throes of their anger and chagrin their one consoling reflection was that no friends less tried than Mr. and Mrs. Rentoul happened to be there to witness their confusion. Yet other sufferers since Job have found that the oldest friends do not necessarily offer the most acceptable consolation.

" Oh, oh ! I feel like to die of grief! " wailed poor Mrs. Gallosh.

" Aye ; it's an awful smack in the eye for you," said Mr. Rentoul sagely.

" Smack in the eye! " thundered his host. " It's a 244
criminal offence—that's what it is! It's a damned swindle! It's a "

" Oh, hush, hush!" interrupted Mrs. Rentoul in a shocked voice. " What words for a lady to hear! After all, you must remember you never made any inquiries."

" Inquiries! What for should I be making inquiries about my guests? You never dropped a word of such a thing! Who'd have listened if I had? It was just Lord Tulliwuddle this and Lord Tulliwuddle that from morning to night since ever he came to the Castle."

" Duncan's so simple-minded," groaned Mrs. Gallosh.

" And what were you, I'd like to know ? What were you?" retorted her justly incensed spouse. "Never a word did I hear, but just that he was such an aristocratic young man, and any one could see he had bluQ blood in his veins, and stuff of that kind! "

" I more than once had my own doubts about that," said the alcohol expert with a knowing wink. " There
was something about him Ah, well, he was not
exactly my own idea of a lord."

" Your idea? " scoffed his oldest and best of friends. " What do you know of lords, I'd like to know ? "

" Well, well," answered the sage peaceably, " maybe we've neither of us had much opportunity of judging of the nobility. It's just more bad luck than anything else that you should have gone to the expense of setting up in style in a lord's castle and then having this downcome. If I'd had similar ambeetions it might have been me."

COUNT BUNKER

This soft answer was so far from turning away wrath, that Mrs. Rentoul again felt compelled to stem the tide of her host's eloquence.

" Oh, hush! " she exclaimed; " I'd have fancied you'd be having no thoughts beyond your daughter's affliction."

' " My Eva! my poor Eva! Where is the suffering child? " cried Mrs. Gallosh. " Duncan, what'll she be doing?"

" Making a to-do like the rest of the women-folk," replied her husband, with rather less sympathy than the occasion seemed to demand.

In point of fact Eva had disappeared from the company immediately after hearing the contents of Mr. Maddison's letter, and whatever she had been doing, it had not been weeping alone, for at that moment she ran into the room, her face agitated, but rather, it seemed, with excitement than grief.

" Papa, lend me five pounds," she panted.

" Lend you—five pounds! And what for, I'd like to know?"

" Don't ask me now. I— I promise to tell you later —some time later."

" I'll see myself ! I mean, you're talking nonsense."

Eva's lip trembled.

"Hi, hist! Eva, my dear," said Mr. Rentoul; "if you're wanting the money badly, and your papa doesn't see his way "

He concluded his sentence with a wink and a dive into his trousers-pocket, and a minute later Eva had fled from the room again.

This action of the sage, being at total variance to his ordinary habits (which indeed erred on the economical side), was attributed by his irate host—with a certain show of reason—to the mere intention of annoying him; and the conversation took a more acrimonious turn than ever. In fact, when Eva returned a few minutes later she was just in time to hear her father thunder in an infuriated voice—

" A German waiter, is he ? Aye, that's verra probable, verra probable indeed. In fact I might have known it when I saw you and him swilling a bottle and a half of my best port together! Birds of a feather —aye, aye, exactly! "

The crushing retort which the sage evidently had ready to heap upon the fire of this controversy was anticipated by Miss Gallosh.

" He isn't a German waiter, papa! He is a German Baron —and an ambassador, too! "

The four started and stared at her.

" Where did you learn that ? " demanded her father.

" I've been talking to the man who brought the letter, and he says that Lord Tulli—I mean the Baron — declares positively that he is a German nobleman! "

" Tuts, fiddlesticks! " scoffed her father.

" Verra like a whale," pronounced the sage.

" I wouldn't believe what "he said," declared Mrs. Gallosh.

" One can see he isn't," said Mrs. Rentoul.

" The kind of Baron that plays in a German band, perhaps," added her husband, with a whole series of winks to give point to this mot.

" He's just a scoundrelly adventurer!" shouted Mr. Gallosh.

" I hope he'll get penal servitude, that's what I hope," said his wife with a sob.

" And, judging from his appearance, that'll be no new experience for him," commented the sage.

So remarkably had their judgment of the late Lord Tulliwuddle waxed in discrimination. And, strange to say, his only defender was the lady he had injured most.

" I still believe him a gentleman!" she cried, and swept tearfully from the room.

WHILE his late worshippers were trampling his memory in the mire, the Baron von Blitzenberg, deserted and dejected, his face still buried in his hands, endured the slow passage of the doleful afternoon. Unlike the prisoner at The Lash, who, by a coincidence that happily illustrates the dispensations of Providence, was undergoing at the same moment an identical ordeal, the Baron had no optimistic, whimsical philosophy to fall back upon. Instead, he had a most tender sense of personal dignity that had been egregiously outraged—and also a wife. Indeed, the thought of Alicia and of Alicia's parent was alone enough to keep his head bowed down.

" Ach, zey most not know," he muttered. " I shall give moch money—hondreds of pound—not to let zem find out. Oh, what for fool have I been! "

So deeply was he plunged in these sorrowful meditations, and so constantly were they concerned with the two ladies whose feelings he wished to spare, that when a hum of voices reached his ear, one of them strangely —even ominously —familiar, he only thought at first that his imagination had grown morbidly vivid. To dispel the unpleasant fancies suggested by this imagined voice, he raised his head, and then the next instant bounded from his chair.

" Mein Gott! " he muttered, " it is she."

Too thunderstruck to move, he saw his prison door open, and there, behold! stood the Countess of Grillyer, a terrible look upon her high-born features, a Darius at either shoulder. In silence they surveyed one another, and it was Mr. Maddison who spoke first.

" Guess this is a friend of yours," he observed.

One thought and one only filled the prisoner's mind —she must leave him, and immediately.

" No, no; I do not know her!" he cried.

"You do not know me?" repeated the Countess in a voice rich in promise.

" Certainly I do not."

" She knows you all right," said the millionaire.

" Says she does," put in Ri in a lower voice; " but I wouldn't lay much money on her word either."

"Rudolph! You pretend you do not know me?" cried the Countess between wrath and bewilderment.

" I never did ever see sochlike a voman before," reiterated the Baron.

"What do you say to that, ma'am?" inquired Mr. Maddison.

" I say—I blush to say—that this wretched young man is my son-in-law," declared the Countess.

As she had come to the house inquiring merely for Lord Tulliwuddle, and been conducted straight to the prisoner's cell, the stupefying effect of this announcement may readily be conceived.

"What!" ejaculated the Dariuses.

" It is not true! She is mad! Take her avay, please!" shouted the Baron, now desperate in his resolution to say or do anything, so long as he got rid of his formidable relative.

The Countess staggered back.

"Is he demented?" she inquired.

"Say, ma'am," put in Ri, "are you the mother of Miss Constance Herringay?"

"Of? I am Lady Grillyer!"

"See here, my good lady, that's going a little too far," said the millionaire not unkindly. "This friend of yours here first calls himself Lord Tulli-wuddle, and then the Baron von something or other. Well, now, that's two of the aristocracy in this undersized apartment already. There's hardly room for a third—see? Can't you be plain Mrs. Smith for a change?"

The Countess tottered.

"Fellow!" she said in a faint voice, "I—I do not understand you."

"Thought that would fetch her down," commented Ri.

"Lead her back to ze train and make her go to London!" pleaded the Baron earnestly.

"You stick to it, you don't know her?" asked Mr. Maddison shrewdly.

"No, no, I do not!"

"Is her name Lady Grillyer?"

"Not more zan it is mine!"

"Rudolph!" gasped the Countess inarticulately. "He is—he was my son!"

"Stoff and nonsense!" roared the Baron. "Remove her!—I am tired."

"Well," said Mr. Maddison, "I guess I don't much believe either of you; but whether you know each other or not, you make such a remarkably fine couple that I reckon you'd better get acquainted now. Come, Ri."

And before either Countess or Baron could interpose, their captors had slipped out, the key was turned, and they were left to the dual enjoyment of the antique apartment.

"Teufel!" shouted the Baron, kicking the door frantically. "Open him, open him! I vill pay you a hondred pound! Goddam! Open!"

But only the gasps of the Countess answered him.

It is generally conceded that if you want to see the full depths of brutality latent in man, you must thoroughly frighten him first. This condition the Countess of Grillyer had exactly succeeded in fulfilling, with the consequence that the Baron, hitherto the most complacent and amiable of sons-in-law, seemed ambitious of rivalling the Turk. When he perceived that no answer to his appeals was forthcoming, dark despair for a moment overcame him. Then the fiendishly ingenious idea struck him—might not a woman's screams accomplish what his own lungs were unable to effect? Turning an inflamed and frowning countenance upon the lady who had intrusted her daughter's happiness to his hands, he addressed her in a deep hissing voice—

"Shcream, shcream, voman! Shcream loudly, or I vill knock you!"

But the Countess was made of stern stuff. Outraged and frightened though she was, she yet retorted huskily—

"I will not scream, Rudolph! I—I demand an explanation first!"

Executing a step of the sword-dance within a yard of her, he reiterated—

"Shcream so zat zey may come back!"

She blinked, but held her ground.

"I insist upon knowing what you mean, Rudolph! I insist upon your telling me! What are you doing here in that preposterous kilt?"

The Baron's wits brightened with the acuteness of the emergency.

"Ha!" he cried, "I vill take my kilt off—take him off before your eyes this instant if you do not shcream!"

But she merely closed her eyes.

"If you dare! If you dare, Rudolph, I shall inform your Emperor! And I will not look! I cannot see you!"

Whether in deference to imperial prejudices, or because a kiltless man would be thrown away upon a lady who refused to look at him, the Baron regretfully desisted from this project. At his wits' end, he besought her —

"Make zem take you avay, so zat you vill be safe from my rage! I do not trost myself mit you. I am so violent as a bull! Better zat you should go; far better—do you not see?"

"No, Rudolph, no!" replied the adamant lady. "I have come to guard you against your own abandoned nature, and I shall only leave this room when you do!"

She sat down and faced him, palpitating, but immovable; and against such obstinacy the unhappy Rudolph gave up the contest in despair.

"But I shall not talk mit her; oh, Himmel, nein!" he said to himself; and in pursuance of this policy sat with his back turned to her while the shadows of evening gradually filled the room. In vain did she address him: he neither answered nor moved. Indeed, to discourage her still further, he even summoned up a forced gaiety of demeanor, and in a low rumble of discords sang to himself the least respectable songs he knew.

"His mind is certainly deranged," thought the Countess. "I must not let him out of my sight. Ah, poor Alicia!"

But in time, when the dusk was thickening so fast that her son-in-law's broad back had already grown indistinct of outline, and no voice or footstep had come near their prison, her thoughts began to wander from his case to her own. The outrageous conduct of those Americans in discrediting her word and incarcerating her person, though overshadowed at the time by the yet greater atrocity of the Baron's behavior, now loomed up in formidable proportions. And the gravity of their offence was emphasized by an unpleasant sensation she now began to experience with considerable acuteness.

"Do they mean to starve us as well as insult us?" she wondered.

The Baron's thoughts also seemed to have drifted into a different channel. He no longer sang; he fidgeted in his chair; he even softly groaned; and at last he actually changed his attitude so far as to survey the dim form of his mother-in-law over one shoulder.

"Oh, ze devil!" he exclaimed aloud. "I am so hongry!"

"That is no reason why you should also be profane," said the Countess severely.

"I did not speak to you," retorted the Baron, and again a constrained silence fell on the room.

The Baron was the first to break it.

"Ha!" he cried. "I hear a step."

"Thank God!" exclaimed the Countess devoutly.

In the blaze of a stable lantern there entered to them Dugald M'Culloch, jailor.

"Will you be for any supper?" he inquired, with a politeness he felt due to prisoners with purses.

"I do starve!" replied the Baron.

"And I am nearly fainting!" cried the Countess.

Both rose with an alacrity astonishing in people so nearly exhausted, and made as though they would pass out. With a deprecatory gesture Dugald arrested them.

"I will bring your supper fery soon," said he.

"Here?" gasped the Countess.

" It is the master's orders."

" Tell him I vill have him ponished mit ze law, if he does not let me come out!" roared the Baron.

Their jailor was courtesy itself; but it was in their prison that they supped—a silent meal, and very plain. And, bitterest pill of all, they were further informed that in their prison they must pass the night.

" In ze same room!" cried the Baron frantically. " Impossible! Improper! "

Even his mother-in-law's solicitude shrank from this vigil; but with unruffled consideration for their comfort their guardian and his assistants made up two beds forthwith. The Baron, subdued to a fierce and snarling moodiness, watched their preparations with a lurid eye.

" Put not zat bed so near ze door," he snapped.

In his ear his jailor whispered, " That one's for you, sir, and dinna put off your clothes!"

The Baron started, and from that moment his air of resignation began to affront the Countess as deeply as his previous violence. When they were again alone, stretched in black darkness each upon their couch, she lifted up her voice in a last word of protest—

" Rudolph! have you no single feeling for me left ? Why didn't you stab that man? "

But the Baron merely retorted with a lifelike affectation of snoring.

CHAPTER XXXVI

FOR a long time the Baron lay wide awake, every sense alert, listening for the creak of a footstep on the wooden stair that led up from the harness-room to his prison. What else could the strange words of Dugald have meant, save that some friend proposed to climb those stairs and gently open that stubborn door? And in this opinion he had been confirmed when he observed that on Dugald's departure the key turned with a silence suggesting a recently oiled lock. His bed lay along the wall, with the head so close to the door that any one opening it and stretching forth a hand could tweak him by the nose without an effort (supposing that were the object of their visit). Clearly, he thought, it was not thus arranged without some very special purpose. Yet when hour after hour passed and nothing happened, he began to sleep fitfully, and at last, worn out with fruitless waiting, dropped into a profound slumber.

He was in the midst of a harassing dream or drama, wherein Bunker and Eva played an incoherent part and he himself passed wearily from peril to peril, when the stage suddenly was cleared, his eyes started open, and he became wakefully conscious of a little ray of light that fell upon his face. Before he could raise his head a soft voice whispered urgently,

"Don't move!"

With admirable self-control he obeyed implicitly.

" Who is zere? " he whispered back.

The voice seemed for a moment to hesitate, and then answered—

" Eleanor Maddison ! "

He started so audibly that again she breathed peremptorily—

" Hush! Lie still till I come back. You — you don't deserve it, but I want to save you from the disgrace of arrest."

" Ach, zank you—mine better angel! " he murmured, with a fervor that seemed not unpleasing to his rescuer.

" You really are a nobleman in trouble ? "

" I swear I am! "

66 And didn't mean anything really wrong?"

"Never—oh, never!"

More kindly than before she murmured—

"Well, I guess I'll take you out, then. I've bribed Dugald, so that's all right. When my car's ready I'll send him up for you. You just lie still till he comes."

From which it appears that Count Bunker's appreciation of the sex fell short of their meed.

Hardly daring to breathe for fear of awakening his fellow-prisoner, trembling with agitation, and consumed by a mad impatience for action, the Baron passed five of the longest minutes he had ever endured.

At the end of that time he heard a stealthy step upon the stairs, and with infinite precautions threw off his bedclothes and sat upright, ready for instant departure. But how slowly and with what a superfluity of precaution his jailor moved! When the door at length opened he wondered that no ray of light fell this time.

"Dugald!" he whispered eagerly.

"Hush!" replied a softer voice than Dugald's; as soft, indeed, as Eleanor's, yet clearly different.

"Who is zat?" he gasped.

"Eva Gallosh!" said the silken voice. "Oh, is that you?"

"Yes—yes—it is me."

"And are you really a Baron and an ambassador?"

"Oh yes—yes—certainly I am."

"Then—then I've come to help you to escape! I've bribed Dugald—and I've got a dog-cart here. Come quickly—but oh, be very quiet!"

For a moment the Baron actually hesitated to flee from that loathed apartment. It seemed to him that if Fortune desired to provide him with opportunities of escape she might have had the sense to offer these one at a time. For how could he tell which of these overtures to close with? A wrong decision might be fatal; yet time unquestionably pressed.

"Mein Gott!" he muttered irresolutely, "vich shall I do?"

At that moment the other bed creaked, and, to his infinite horror, he heard a suspicious voice demand—

"Is that you talking, Rudolph?"

Poor Eva, who was quite unaware of the presence of another prisoner, uttered a stifled shriek; with a cry of "Fly, quickly!" the Baron leaped from his bed, and headlong down the wooden stairs they clattered for freedom.

A dim vision of the thrice-bribed Dugald, screeching, "The car's ready for ye, sir!" but increased their speed.

Outside, a motor car stood panting by the door, and in the youthful driver, turning a pale face toward them in the lamp's radiance, the Baron had just time to recognize his first fair deliverer.

"Good-bye!" he whispered to his second, and flung himself in.

Some one followed him; the door was slammed, and with a mighty throbbing they began to move.

"Rudolph! Rudolph!" wailed a voice behind them.

"Zank ze goodness she is not here!" exclaimed the Baron.

"Whisht! whisht!" he could hear Dugald expostulate.

With a violent start he turned to the fellow-passenger who had followed him in.

" Are you not Dugald ? " he demanded hoarsely.

" No—it's—it's me! I dursn't wait for my dogcart!"

"Eva!" he murmured. "Oh, Himmel! Vat shaU I do?"

Only a screen of glass separated his two rescuers, and the one had but to turn her head and look inside, or the other to study with any attention the roll of hair beneath their driver's cap, in order to lead to most embarrassing consequences. Not that it was his fault he should receive such universal sympathy: but would these charming ladies admit his innocence?

" How thoughtful of Dugald to have this car " began Eva.

" Hush !" he muttered hoarsely. " Yes, it was thoughtful, but you most not speak too loudly."

" For fear ? " she smiled, and turned her eyes instinctively toward their driver.

" Excuse me," he muttered, sweeping her as gently as possible from her seat and placing her upon the floor.

" It vill not do for zem to see you," he explained in a whisper.

" How awful a position," he reflected. " Oh, I hope it may still be dark ven we get to ze station."

But with rising concern he presently perceived that the telegraph posts along the roadside were certainly grown plainer already; he could even see the two thin wires against a paling sky; the road behind was visible for half a mile; the hill-tops might no longer be confounded with the clouds—day indubitably was breaking. Also he recollected that to go from Lincoln Lodge to Torrydhulish Station one had to make a vast detour round half the loch; and, further, began to suspect that though Miss Maddison's driving was beyond reproach her knowledge of topography was

COUNT BUNKER

scarcely so dependable. In point of fact she increased the distance by at least a third, and all the while day was breaking more fatally clear.

To discourage Miss Gallosh's efforts at conversation, yet keep her sitting contentedly upon the floor; to appear asleep whenever Miss Maddison turned her head and threw a glance inside, and to devise some adequate explanation against the inevitable discovery at the end of their drive, provided him with employment worthy of a diplomatist's steel. But now, at last, they were within sight of railway signals and a long embankment; and over a pine wood a stream of smoke moved with a swelling roar. Then into plain view broke the engine and carriage after carriage racing behind. Regardless of risk, he leaped from his seat and flung up the window, crying—

" Ach, look! Ve shall be late! "

" That train is going north," said Eleanor. " Guess we've half an hour good before yours comes in."

So little can mortals read the stars that he heaved a sigh of relief, and even murmured—

" Ve have timed him very luckily! "

Ten minutes later they descended the hill to Torry-dhulish Station. The north-going train had paid its brief call and vanished nearly from sight again ; no one seemed to be moving about the station, and the Baron told himself that nothing worse remained than the exercise of a little tact in parting with his deliverers.

leaping lightly to the ground, exclaimed with a genial air, as he gave his hand to Eva—

" Veil ! Now have I a leetle surprise for you, ladies!"

Nor did he at all exaggerate their sensation.

" Miss Maddison! "

Alas, that it should be so far beyond the power of mere inky words to express all that was implied in Eva's accents!

"Miss Gallosh!"

Nor is it less impossible to supply the significance of Eleanor's intonation.

" Ladies, ladies! " he implored, " do not, I pray you, misunderstand! I vas not responsible—I could not help it. You both vould come mit me! No, no, do not look so at me! I mean not zat—I mean I could not do vizout both of you. Ach, Himmel! Vat do I say ? I should say zat—zat "

He broke off with a start of apprehension.

" Look! Zere comes a man mit a bicycle! Zis is too public! Come mit me into ze station and I shall eggsplain! He waves his fist! Come! you vould not be seen here? "

He offered one arm to Eva, the other to Eleanor; and so alarming were the gesticulations of the approaching cyclist, and so beseeching the Baron's tones, that without more ado they clung to him and hurried on to the platform.

" Come to ze vaiting-room! " he whispered. " Zere shall ve be safe! "

Alack for the luck of the Baron von Blitzenberg! Out of the very door they were approaching stepped a solitary lady, sole passenger from the south train, and at the sight of those three, linked arm in arm, she staggered back and uttered a cry more piercing than the engine's distant whistle.

"Rudolph!" cried this lady.

" Alicia! " gasped the Baron.

His rescuers said nothing, but clung to him the more tightly, while in the Baroness's startled eyes a harder light began to blaze.

"Who are these, Rudolph?"

He cleared his throat, but the process seemed to take some time, and in the meanwhile he felt the grip of his deliverers relax.

"Who is that lady?" demanded Eleanor.

" His wife," replied the Baroness.

The Baron felt his arms freed now; but still his Alicia waited an answer. It came at last, but not from the Baron's lips.

" Well, here you all are! " said a cheerful voice behind them.

CHAPTER XXXVII

THEY turned as though they expected to see an apparition. Nor was the appearance of the speaker calculated to disappoint such expectations. Their startled eyes beheld indeed the most remarkable figure that had ever wheeled a bicycle down the platform of Torrydhulish Station. Hatless, in evening clothes with blue lapels upon the coat, splashed liberally with mud, his feet equipped only with embroidered socks and saturated pumps, his shirt-front bestarred with souvenirs of all the soils for thirty miles, Count Bunker made a picture that lived long in their memories. Yet no foolish consciousness of his plight disturbed him as he addressed the Baron.

" Thank you, Baron, for escorting my fair friends so far. I shall now take them off your hands."

He smiled with pleasant familiarity upon the two astonished girls, and then started as though for the first time he recognized the Baroness.

" Baroness ! " he cried, bowing profoundly, " this is a very unexpected pleasure! You came by the early train, I presume? A tiresome journey, isn't it?"

But bewilderment and suspicion were all that he could read in reply.

" What — what are you doing here ? "

COUNT BUNKER

lie was not in the least disconcerted.

" Meeting my cousins" (he indicated the Misses Gallosh and Maddison with an amiable glance), " whom the Baron has been kind enough to look after till my arrival."

Audaciously approaching more closely, he added, in a voice intended for her ear and the Baron's alone—

" I must throw myself, I see, upon your mercy, and ask you not to tell any tales out of school. Cousins, you know, don't always want their meetings advertised—do they, Baron ? "

Alicia's eyes softened a little.

" Then, they are really your "

" Call 'em cousins, please! I have your pledge that you won't tell? Ah, Baron, your charming wife and I understand one another."

Then raising his voice for the benefit of the company generally—

" Well, you two will want to have a little talk in the waiting-room, I've no doubt. We shall pace the platform. Very fit Rudolph's looking, isn't he, Baroness? You've no idea how his lungs have strengthened."

" His lungs!" exclaimed the Baroness in a changed voice.

Giving the Baron a wink to indicate that there lay the ace of trumps, he answered reassuringly—

" When you learn how he has improved you'll forgive me, I'm sure, for taking him on this little trip. Well, see you somewhere down the line, no doubt—I'm going by the same train."

He watched them pass into the waiting-room, and then turned an altered face to the two dumbfounded girls. It was expressive now solely of sympathy and contrition.

" Let us walk a little this way," he began, and thus having removed them safely from earshot of the waiting-room door, he addressed himself to the severest part of his task.

" My dear girls, I owe you I don't know how many apologies for presuming to claim you as my friends. The acuteness of the emergency is my only excuse, and I throw myself most contritely upon your mercy!"

This second projection of himself upon a lady's mercy proved as successful as the first.

" Well," said Eleanor slowly, " I guess maybe we can forgive you for that; but what I want to know is—what's happened?—who's who?—and where just exactly are we? "

" That's just what I want to know too," added Eva sadly.

Indeed, they both had a hint of tears in their eyes, and in their voices.

" What has happened," replied the Count, " is that a couple of thoughtless masqueraders came up here to play a little joke, and succeeded in getting themselves into a scrape. For your share in getting us out of it we cannot feel too grateful."

" But, who is ? " the girls began together, and

then stopped, with a rise of color and a suspicion of displeasure in their interchange of eyes.

" Who is who ? Well, my friend is the Baron von Blitzenberg; and the lady is, as she stated, his wife."

" Then all this time " began Eva.

" He was married! " Eleanor finished for her. " Oh, the heartless scoundrel! To think that I rescued him! "

" I wouldn't have either! " said Eva ; " I mean if— if I had known he treated you so badly."

" Treated me! I was only thinking of you, Miss Gallosh!"

" Dear ladies! " interposed the Count with his ready tact, " remember his excuse."

"His excuse?"

" The beauty, the charm, the wit of the lady who took by storm a heart not easily captured! He himself, poor fellow, thought it love-proof; but he had not then met her. Think mercifully of him! "

He was so careful to give no indication which of the rival belles was " her," that each was able to take to herself a certain mournful consolation.

" That wasn't much excuse," said Eleanor, yet with a less vindictive air.

" Certainly not very much," murmured Eva.

" He ought to have thought of the pain he was giving her" added Eleanor.

" Yes," said Eva. " Indeed he ought! "

"Yes, that is true," allowed the Count; "but remember his punishment! To be married already now proves to be less his fault than his misfortune."

By this time he had insidiously led them back to their car.

" And must you return at once ? " he exclaimed.

" We had better," said Eleanor, with a suspicion of a sigh. " Miss Gallosh, I'll drive you home first."

" You're too kind, Miss Maddison."

"Oh, no!"

The Count assisted them in, greatly pleased to see this amicable spirit. Then shaking hands heartily with each, he said—

" I can speak for my friend with conviction, because my own regard for the lady in question is as deep and as sincere as his. Believe me, I shall never forget her!"

He was rewarded with two of the kindest smiles ever bestowed upon him, and as they drove away each secretly wondered why she had previously preferred the Baron to the Count. It seemed a singular folly.

" Two deuced nice girls," mused he; "I do believe I told 'em the truth in every particular! "

He watched their car dwindle to a scurrying speck, and then strolled back thoughtfully to purchase his ticket.

He found the signals down, and the far-off clatter of the train distinctly audible through the early morning air. A few minutes more and he was stepping into a first-class compartment, his remarkable costume earning (he could not but observe) the pronounced attention of the guard. The Baron and Alicia, with an air of mutual affection, entered another; both the doors were closed, everything seemed ready, yet the train lingered.

" Start ze train! Start ze train! I vill give you a pound—two pound—tree pound, to start him! "

The Count leaped up and thrust his head through the window.

"What the dickens ! " thought he.

Hanging out of the other window he beheld the clamant Baron urging the guard with frenzied entreaty.

" But they're wanting to go by the train, sir," said the guard.

" No, no. Zey do not! It is a mistake! Start him!"

Following their gaze he saw, racing toward them, the cause of their delay. It was a motor car, yet not the same that had so lately departed. In this were seated a young man and an elderly lady, both waving to hold back the train; and to his vast amazement he recognized in the man Darius Maddison, junior, in the lady the Countess of Grillyer.

The car stopped, the occupants alighted, and the Countess, supported on the strong arm of Ri, scuttled down the platform.

" Bonker, take her in mit you! " groaned the Baron, and his head vanished from the Count's sight.

Even this ordeal was not too much for Bunker's fidelity.

" Madam, there is room here! " he announced politely, as they swept past; but with set faces they panted toward the doomed von Blitzenberg.

All of the tragedy that the Count, with strained neck, could see or overhear, was a vision of the Countess being pushed by the guard and her escort into that first-class compartment whence so lately the Baron's crimson visage had protruded, and the voice of Ri stridently declaring—•

" Guess you'll recognize your momma this time, Baron!"

A whistle from the guard, another from the engine, and they were off, clattering southward in the first of the morning sunshine.

Inadequately attired, damp, hungry, and divorced from tobacco as the Count was, he yet could say to himself with the sincerest honesty—

" I wouldn't change carriages with the Baron von Blitzenberg—not even for a pair of dry socks and a cigar! Alas, poor Rudolph! May this teach all young men a lesson in sobriety of conduct! "

For which moral reflection the historian feels it incumbent upon him, as a philosopher and serious psychologist, to express his conscientious admiration.

EPILOGUE

IT was an evening in early August, luminous and warm; the scene, a certain club now emptied of all but a sprinkling of its members; the festival, dinner; and the persons of the play, that gentleman lately known as Count Bunker and his friend the Baron von Blitzenberg. The Count was habited in tweeds; the Baron in evening dress.

" It vas good of you to come up to town jost to see me," said the Baron.

" I'd have crossed Europe, Baron! "

The Baron smiled faintly. Evidently he was scarcely in his most florid humor.

" I vish I could have asked you to my club, Bonker."

" Are you dissatisfied with mine ? "

" Oh, no, no! But veil, ze fact is, it vould be reported by some one if I took you to ze Regents. Bonker, she does have me watched! "

"The Baroness?"

" Her mozzer."

"The deuce, Baron!"

The diplomatist gloomily sipped his wine.

" You did hush it all up, eh? " he inquired presently.

" Completely."

" Zank you. I vas so afraid of some scandal !" 272

" So were they; that's where I had 'em.'*

" Did zey write in moch anger ? "

" No —not very much; rather nice letters, in fact."

The Baron began to cheer up.

" Ach, so! Vas zere any news of—ze Galloshes ? "

" Yes, they seem very well. Old Rentoul has caught a salmon. Gallosh hopes to get a fair bag "

" Bot did zey say nozing about—about Miss Eva? "

" The letter was written by her, you see."

" She wrote to you! Strange! "

"Very odd, isn't it?"

The Baron meditated for a minute and then inquired—

" Vat of ze Maddisons? "

" Well, I gather that Mr. Maddison is erecting an ibis house in connection with the aviary. Ri has gone to Kamchatka, but hopes to be back by the 12th "

" And Eleanor—no vord of her? "

" It was she who wrote, don't you know."

" Eleanor—and also to you! Bot vy should she?"

" Can't imagine; can you ? "

The Baron shook his head solemnly. " No, Bonker, I cannot."

For some moments he pondered over the remarkable conduct of these ladies; and then—

"Did you also hear of ze Wallingfords ?" he asked.

" I had a short note from them."

" From him, or "

" Her."

COUNT BUNKER

" So! Humph, zey all seem fond of writing letters."

" Why—have you had any too? "

" No; and I do not vant zem."

Yet his immunity did not appear to exhilarate the diplomatist.

" Another bottle of the same," said Bunker aside to the waiter.

• •••••

It was an hour later; the scene and the personages the same, but the atmosphere marvellously altered.

" To ze ladies, Bonker! "

"To her, Baron!"

"To zem both!"

The genial heart, the magnanimous soul of Rudolph von Blitzenberg had asserted their dominion again. Depression, jealousy, repentance, qualms, and all other shackles of the spirit whatsoever, had fled discomfited. Now at last he saw his late exploits in their true heroic proportions, and realized his marvellous good fortune in satisfying his aspirations so gloriously. Raising his glass once more, he cried—

" Dear Bonker, my heart he does go out to you! !Ach, you have given me soch a treat. Vunce more I schmell ze mountain dew— I hear ze pipes— I gaze into loffly eyes— I am ze noblest part of mineself! Bonker, I vill defy ze mozzer of my wife! I drink to you, my friend, mit hip—hip—hip— hooray! "

" You have more than repaid me," replied the Count, "by the spectacle you have provided. Dear Baron, it was a panorama calculated to convert a continent!"

" To vat should it convert him? " inquired the Baron with interest.

" To a creed even merrier than Socialism, more convivial than Total Abstinence, and more perfectly designed for human needs than Esperanto—the gospel of * Cheer up.' "

" Sheerup ? " repeated the Baron, whose acquaint1 ance with the English words used in commerce and war was singularly intimate, but who was occasionally at fault with terms of less portentous import.

" A name given to the bridge that crosses the Slough of Despond," explained the Count.

The Baron still seemed puzzled. " I am not any wiser," said he.

" Never cease thanking Heaven for that!" cried Bunker fervently. " The man who once dubs himself wise is the jest of gods and the plague of mortals."

With this handsome tribute to the character and attainments of one of these heroes, and the Baronial roar that congratulated the other, our chronicle may fittingly leave them; since the mutual admiration of two such catholic critics is surely more significant than the colder approval of a mere historian.

THE END